The BOOK of
ELEANOR

NAT BURNS

Bella
BOOKS
2012

Bella Books, Inc.
P.O. Box 10543
Tallahassee, FL 32302

Printed in the United States of America on acid-free paper
First published 2012

Editor: Nene Adams
Cover Designer: Linda Callaghan

ISBN 13: 978-1-59493-309-7

Other Bella Books by Nat Burns

Two Weeks in August
House of Cards
The Quality of Blue
Identity

Acknowledgment

I sincerely thank the lovely people of Port Isabel, Texas. And I do apologize for the literary license I took implying that their spectacular fishing village is haunted and that some of the officials are mean. Port Isabel is haunted maybe but mean, never.

Also, many thanks to editor, Nene Adams, for the editing sweep that tightened up my careless construction. And to Karin Kallmaker at Bella, for her endless encouragement and support.

Dedication

I'd like to dedicate this book to my Aunt Jean who just adores a good ghost story. And for dearest Chris, who doesn't adore them at all, but bravely read several versions of this manuscript anyway.

About the Author

Nat Burns' job titles have included:
-Staff reporter (three VPA Awards)
-Media coordinator (tourism writer)
-Technical support (for a software company)
-Editorial systems coordinator (for a Washington DC publishing firm)
-Teacher and support staff (in local school systems)
-Board member (of Literacy Volunteers of America, Nelson County Education Foundation, Golden Crown Literary Society and the Small Press Writers and Artists Organization)
-Novelist and editor.

Currently she lives in New Mexico, writing and editing full time. *www.natburns.com.*

ANGIE

As soon as I laid eyes on her, I knew she was the one meant for me. And it wasn't just a physical thing, although she was *fine*, if you know what I mean. No, it was something about her aura. Yeah, aura. I know, *I know*. Angie June is not usually guilty of using the gift that way. I try mighty hard to fit in and turn a blind eye to all that extra occult info I pick up. And for the record, all those allegations of weirdness, dancing naked in the moonlight and all, are false. Most were spread by my ex, Cathy. She just loves gossip and will make it up if what's already going around isn't quite juicy enough.

So what I saw when I looked close was the peaceful sadness of the woman's aura. It drew me. She had a certain fragility that made me want to pull her close and protect her, like my kids at the center. Not helpless, though. No, not helpless. There was a power huddling inside her that intrigued me and made me curious.

The woman had taken a seat at the table just inside the door. That alone let me know she was a newcomer. Out-of-towners always sat from the door inward while the locals fanned out from the bar in the front. I wasn't sure why visitors were so apprehensive. Perhaps they wanted a quick escape if they hated Mama's food. Or wanted to run out on the bill. That had happened before.

Besides, she had to be new to the area. I would have remembered her if she'd been here before. Delicate and slender, she had an amazingly beautiful face, dynamic enough to be a model. I could just imagine her in some big-name magazine, modeling the latest trends in makeup and fashion. Her blond hair hung just past her shoulders and had the kind of metallic sleekness that always fascinated me. How did some women get their hair to lie so smoothly, so perfectly? My short, choppy hair never behaved. I did have the sun and wind to contend with, but even so, I dreamed of having glossy, well-behaved hair.

I fingered my abused locks absently as I hid behind the swinging kitchen doors peering through one of the small, octagonal windows set into each door. I'd retreated there after spying her from behind the bar. I wanted to watch her without being seen, but I knew that as soon as an order came through, I'd be busted. Still, I watched her, completely captivated.

The beautiful woman also dressed like a model. In an area where baggy cargo shorts and T-shirts were considered the norm, she wore a thin, jade-green mock turtleneck, sleeveless, over tight jeans which flared out gracefully over strappy heels.

Heels? I practically salivated. No one wore heels in Port Isabel except the Mexican girls who loved to dress up. Even the

Winter Texans considered themselves here on vacation and wore sandals or bright white athletic shoes. No, she had to be visiting for the day, maybe a saleswoman from some big city north of here. Houston, San Antonio, or maybe even Dallas. I tried to place her vocation. Real estate? That was the big mover and shaker around here. I watched for clues as she tilted her head over the menu.

Sudden embarrassment flooded me. Why hadn't we upgraded those menus last month when we'd talked about it? Most of them were pretty shabby. I chewed my thumbnail. Well, at least the food here was some of the best in Port Isabel and, many said, even South Padre Island.

I sighed while I studied her. If she lived far away, how would we manage to become a couple? Weird how I just knew things, even when they were as impractical as all get out.

The mental images persisted. I saw us together, my head buried in the curve of her neck and her slender arms around me. I gazed deep into her eyes and ran my hands along that tender area on each side of her ribcage, just below the bra line, until she shivered uncontrollably. She turned her sweet face up to me and I...

"Move it, lardass," Hasty growled as he pushed past me, a fragrant basket of bread in one hand and a bowl of roasted garlic and olive oil in the other.

I had a sudden urge to shove my foot into the opposite door's path so it would slap him in the face. The thought of Mama's certain wrath stopped me. Instead, I stuck my tongue out at his oiled Latin ducktail as he retreated.

I took one more glance at the woman, stilling the door so I could see through the small window. Hasty stood above her. He'd turned on the charm. I saw her precious, dimpled smile when she looked up at him with wide eyes. Damn! She was probably straight. Just my luck. Reluctantly, I turned away and moved into the kitchen. Mama, bless her hardworking heart, stood at the deep double sinks rinsing off her favorite mixing bowl.

"Are you out of dough already? We just started on lunch," I said, fishing a slice of green pepper out of the *sous* bins behind the composition line.

Mama looked at me and smiled, a brilliant smile that radiated the happiness of one of the happiest people I knew. "Nope, just gettin' ready. Can you take a pizza over to Melvin? He called and says he's starvin' 'cause the only thing available at the show is popcorn and flatbread, and he ain't goin' for it."

"Sure. Hey, Mama, I found someone finally and she is the perfect one for me," I said, absently twirling the flat oven board on the stainless steel countertop. I jumped when Mama's dough bowl hit the sink. She stared at me with huge, glistening brown eyes. I smiled uncertainly.

"Oh, my God," Mama sighed, laying a hand on her ample chest. "Who is she, baby? I didn't even know you were seeing anyone. We gotta have a party. I'll call Sanchez and she can round up the girls. This is so exciting..." She paused expectantly.

My mother, Maylie Lynn June, who grew up in the bosom of the Louisiana bayou, was big in body and big in spirit, and probably one of the sweetest people imaginable. Until she was riled, of course. But she usually radiated total acceptance and love, thank my lucky stars. As far as I was concerned, just having a child with my special abilities and raising me all alone made her a saint in my eyes.

She also knew everything there was to know about food and had years of successful restauranteering to back up what I, and a good portion of The Point, believed as fact. There was no one, and I repeat, no one, who put more care into producing good Italian fare than my mama.

"Hold up, Mama. She doesn't know yet," I said, putting out a warning hand.

Mama frowned and turned back to the sink to rescue her oversized stainless steel bowl. "Get on with your foolishness, Angie. I am not in the mood." A low chuckle let me know she wasn't seriously miffed.

"No lie, Mama. You gotta come see her."

I took Mama by the upper arm and practically dragged her through the swinging tavern doors and into the area behind the bar. I tried to make out like I was polishing the bar while nodding my head meaningfully in the woman's direction. Mama took the hint and moved some highball glasses around under the counter. Her eyes were fixed on the woman, who looked out the window with her elbow resting on the table and her chin cupped in her palm.

Mama turned wide eyes to me and silently mouthed, "She's pretty."

I nodded and hustled Mama back into the kitchen, scaring the life out of Gail, who was putting together Melvin's pizza. Hasty, getting a salad out of the walk-in fridge, frowned at us. Mama slapped my hands away and stood with her hands on her hips, breathing heavily and glaring at me.

"Did you see it, all around her?" I asked nervously.

"Now, Angie, you know I don't see that stuff like you do. Who is she, though, can you tell?" Mama walked around the buffer over to the kitchen doors. She peered curiously through one of the little windows, much as I had earlier. I was close on her heels.

Hasty poked his head around the buffer. "We need another breakfast pizza, Maylie. Bacon." His glance roved across me and dismissed me outright.

"I really hate him," I said after he walked away. I took Mama's hands in mine. "Listen, I need to touch something. Go get her glass, straw and all," I told her.

She looked at me as if I'd gone daft. "Now, Angie, explain to me what I'm going to tell that paying customer when I go and take her drink away from her."

"I don't know," I let her go, twisting my hands together anxiously. "I just wish I could meet her, is all."

Mama's gaze softened as she studied me. "What do we say around here, Angela Rose?"

I sighed. "If meant to be, it'll be," I said.

Mama pressed a hand to her heart. "Amen. Now, I've got to get back to work and you do too. We got a business to run, baby girl."

She hurried off. I stole a final glance out the small window, then moved to fold a box for Melvin's pie. The harsh sizzle of bacon reached me as Mama worked the grill. It smelled delicious. Gail, over by the huge brick and mortar pizza oven, withdrew a large "everything" pizza with extra green peppers, Melvin's favorite. The pie was cooked to perfection, still bubbling on top. I held out the box and Gail slid the pizza inside.

"You know where he is, right?" she asked.

"Yep, conference center today."

"Mmm hmm, by the front door, south side," she answered, slapping a new lump of dough onto the board.

I tossed in packets of cheese and red pepper flakes and closed the box as I walked toward the kitchen door. I saw that Willie had his ice truck pulled up to the stoop. He was busy unloading, so I waved to him before executing a quick U-turn, excited that I would get to see the woman up close when I passed through the dining room.

I made it all the way through the swinging doors before I felt it. I paused in twisting my car keys out of my pocket, but couldn't stop my feet and their forward motion.

Hasty raced past me toward the kitchen, and then it happened: disaster. Our feet tangled for a brief instant, but it was just enough for him to fall into the kitchen buffer wall and me to pitch headfirst into the woman.

I saw big green eyes widen in surprise as I descended, and all I could think about was *if meant to be, it'll be* when the pizza box exploded, showering us both with hot pizza and colorful packets of condiments.

My right hip hit the table hard, but I ended up sort of in her lap and on the table at the same time. I lay there for a long, shocked moment, watching a slice of Melvin's pizza ooze its way down the front of her shirt. Time seemed to stand still as the woman and I regarded one another. The entire dining room went silent, customers watching in amazement. There was a smear of sauce on her left cheek and a slice of green pepper on one shoulder.

"Are you burnt?" I finally asked when I could speak.

"No," she said, shaking her head slowly. "I ordered the pasta primavera, though, not the pizza."

The hilarity hit me. I slid from the table and onto the floor, laughing. Though limp from merriment, I moved to lift the twisted slices of pizza off her, the table, and the floor. I lifted a silverware setup from a nearby table and used the napkin to mop up as best I could. Her salad had exploded as well, sending lettuce shrapnel everywhere. By some miracle, the bowl of garlic and olive oil rested undisturbed on the table, although the bread basket had tumbled.

I tried not to laugh, but every time I met her twinkling eyes, it set me off again. She kept smiling, thank goodness, and helped straighten up the mess, using a napkin to sweep salad into the pizza box. We worked in silence while the normal restaurant chatter resumed around us.

I fetched another napkin and moved to wipe the sauce from her cheek. Our eyes met. When one of my knuckles touched her soft, cool skin, a swift current ran up my arm. In my vision, her eyes darkened with pain and loss. Grief pressed against my heart, threatening to still it. I pulled back reflexively, glad to see the bright, merry green eyes of this moment return.

"Angie! What in the world?"

I sighed and shrugged at the woman. Mama had heard the ruckus, or maybe the sudden silence, and come to investigate. I turned to her, trying to squelch my overwhelming amusement. It did little good. I answered chuckling.

"I tripped over Hasty and fell...fell into this nice woman here."

Mama turned her attention to the customer and began mopping at her with a dishtowel. It was hopeless, smeared cheese and sauce everywhere. "Oh, Lord, honey, I am so, so very sorry this happened. You listen, we will pay for every bit of this dry cleaning. You just bring the bill right on here and we'll take care of it."

Hasty, too, descended on the customer, promising a new salad and stating that lunch was, of course, on us. He ignored me completely, using his elbows to push me aside as he and Mama hovered. I moved back farther, the crushed box filled with accident debris held to my chest.

I took a deep breath and staggered into the kitchen to clean myself up, haunted by sad jade eyes and filled with remorse because I never thought to get her name.

GREY

After Mary was taken, I found myself wishing for light to shine on me. I was in such a dark place when her daily glow subsided from my life, I worried that I would become, from that point onward, a curved, pale grub buried beneath the soil of my sadness. Heading south toward the sun seemed like a good idea, so I left the Central Texas home we'd shared and moved as far south in the Lone Star State as possible, to endless warmth and brightness.

The welcome sun bathed my face with necessary heat as I stood in a parking area next to the wild, untamed beach of South

Padre Island. I'd checked out of the small Los Fresnos hotel after a restless night, passed right by my new, as yet unexplored, home at Lighthouse Square in Port Isabel, and pushed headlong toward the broad expanse of ocean and unhindered sunlight. There'd be time enough, too much time, I was sure, for dealing with the settling in. What I needed now was the healing energy of water and hot, hot light on my skin.

I walked around my parked car and looked through the partially open passenger window at Oscar Marie. Her cat carrier rested high on a stack of suitcases. Her broad, flat face was pressed against the metal door grate, eyes wide and nose twitching as she took in the unfamiliar sights and smells of beach and ocean.

"Will you be okay for a few minutes?" I asked, reaching through the grate to scratch the heavy black hair around the scruff of her neck. "I'm just going to walk down and put my feet in the water. I'd take you with me, but you wouldn't like it. Too much wind."

She ignored me, but I think it was more curiosity about the noises coming from a nearby hotel than her being miffed at me.

"I'll be back. Stay put and be good."

She looked at me finally, her eyes made golden by the harsh sunlight. She blinked slowly.

Taking this as permission. I slipped my flats from my feet and held them in both hands as I strode onto the hot sand, leaving the towering hotels behind me. I was grateful for the scorch of the sand against my tender feet, which woke senses numbed for the past six months.

I glanced left and right, surprised to see only a handful of beach-goers. The lakes I had frequented in the Dallas area were usually packed shoulder–to–shoulder, even this early in the spring, so the lack of crowds was a refreshing change.

Looking back at my car parked close by in the small, beach access lot, I mentally noted the proximity and walked left, my route moving diagonally toward the water. Roiling waves pounded the sand, which had cooled considerably beneath the soles of my feet. Foam peppered my clothing as I pushed toward the waves, and the rampant, unceasing wind snatched wildly at my unbound hair. I walked a long time in wide, elliptical circles, my mind blank, simply reacting to the environment. Gulls begged loudly above me, and some brave fellows even walked haphazardly beside me, as though I were simply hiding food from them as a tease. A rebel wave soaked the hem of my jeans, and I paused.

I closed my eyes, battling vertigo as I experienced fully the magnitude of the new life I was making for myself. I realized that this place of water perfectly reflected my emotional turmoil. Me, who had real problems trusting others, had, after many years, let down my walls of emotional isolation and loved fully.

Mary had been taken from me brutally, as suddenly as my mother almost two decades earlier. How does one come back from that new betrayal? What kind of cruel universe would allow me to open my wounded self, allow me to lay down my arms, and then attack me anew? My bitterness rankled.

It had been hard selling our home, but harder still to stay there, expecting to find Mary glancing up at me in every room I entered. I was lucky and sold the house quickly, packing what I felt I had to keep, and selling or donating the rest of my old life.

Letting go of Mary's things was not easy. Both her sisters came over while I was closeted in my office working, and thankfully, they handled the bulk. I kept just one of her shirts in the office with me. It still smelled like her, peppery and fierce.

Mary had worked for a company called Fellingworth Art which created and choreographed beautiful firework displays. Pyrotechnics, she called them. I regret to say I never really learned very many details about her job during our ten years living together. She would leave home in the morning, all dewy from her shower, and come home in the evenings grubby and smelling spicy from something she called black powder.

Though I loved going to the many fireworks displays we attended, the points of light on Mary are what fascinated me the most. I will always remember that about her.

The first time I saw this side effect of her job, we'd only been dating about two weeks. We had arranged to meet at a local bar where our mutual friend, Carmen, was performing her stand-up comedy routine. I got there first and cribbed a good table, stage side. I talked with Carmen while I waited, standing between Carmen and the table, and glancing impatiently toward the front door.

Time passed. Carmen left to go backstage, and then, just as the lights dimmed for the show and the spotlights came up, Miss Mary Leigh Banks entered the club. It was the first time I'd seen her come directly from work and I was awed by her beauty.

Although I made out her form, clad in her usual T-shirt and jeans, the metals and chemicals she worked with had created a shimmering cloak of iridescence over her body that took my breath away. Each movement as she crossed the room toward me held me entranced. I could not take my gaze away.

When she approached even closer, I saw that metal powder exquisitely framed her sparkling brown eyes, nestling into and defining each laugh line. Her mouth and cheekbones bore a similar outline. I leaned into her, wishing to take some of that beauty for myself.

Our lips met in our second real kiss as we fell into our seats. I felt Mary's dynamic energy fill me. Was that when I fell in love with her? Maybe. The falling into love was such a gradual, natural thing that it would be hard to pinpoint.

I do know that the next ten years with her would define my life in a brand-new way. Oddly enough, even after her passing, my life was still changing.

Though Mary's sisters helped me deal with the dispersion of most of her possessions, they had not wanted her books. Younger sister Elizabeth wasn't interested. Not surprising since she lives in a small studio apartment in downtown Cedar Springs and works as a busy bankruptcy lawyer. Brynna, the eldest, hemmed and hawed a bit, but eventually asked me to do something with them, perhaps sell them if I could. She did pick out two favorite books that she and Mary had read as children. That still left thousands of volumes for me to deal with.

I paused in my frantic strides on the beach, remembering the first time I'd walked into Mary's library after her death. The room had felt so strange without her in it. She loved books. No, understand me, she *loved* books like most people love air.

I take that back. Air is taken for granted, and Mary would never take a book for granted. Each volume was like a beloved child to her. She knew its name and history without a moment's hesitation. She had collections by specific authors that she liked or stood in awe of, and the books ranged through every genre and every time period. The author collections not only decorated her shelves with hardback first editions, but also trade paperbacks and even cheaply made imports from other countries. She had them all. One of her favorite pastimes was browsing through used bookstores.

It used to annoy me, I admit it. No matter where we were or what we were doing, if there was a bookstore nearby, Mary was in it. She even had her entire collection listed in her BlackBerry, with an additional list of the books she needed to buy to round out her various sub-collections. I can't begin to list the stores I waited outside, reading to pass the time yet growing ever more impatient. I sincerely regret that impatience. Especially now that I am alone and have so many empty hours to fill, knowing she won't return to me.

I may have been able to let go of most of Mary's things but her beloved books...well, I found it impossible to let them go in one fell swoop to some anonymous dealer—a type of guilt, or maybe an apology, I suppose. Thus, I was forced to spend a lot of time pondering what to do with, and how to evaluate, several thousand valuable books.

I wasn't as big a reader as Mary, nor loved the books for their very essence as she had. I did want to keep them close, though. I felt I could, over time, use them in some mysterious way as payback for having been allowed to keep her presence in my life for as long as I did.

After stopping for coffee while running errands one day in Dallas, I'd been surprised to find books scattered around the coffeehouse. I realized it was a reading room as well as a coffee shop. People came in and read while having coffee, but left the books behind where they belonged. I decided such a business would be a perfect venue, providing a way for other book lovers to appreciate and enjoy Mary's collection. She would have been pleased. So the idea for Mary's Bookmark, a combined coffeehouse and reading room, was born.

It was a great way to invest Mary's money as well. I was suddenly and unexpectedly wealthy because Mary, bless her heart, had—unbeknownst to me—named me as beneficiary on her life insurance and retirement accounts at work. In addition, Fellingworth Art generously included me in the customary accidental death benefit they paid to Mary's sisters. Mary and I had been together openly almost eleven years, and they knew we were our own small family.

I think they were actually afraid I would sue them because of the way Mary died. The thought never even crossed my mind until my friend Tara mentioned it. Sure, Fellingworth should have never let a novice employee set two of the charges, but Mary saved his life and that was why she had died that day. Her heroism killed her, not the company's negligence. I would never sully that heroism with a lawsuit.

So I, who had always made a successful living on my own, bolstered by a small nest egg for security, now had the task of managing more than a million dollars. I stared at a trio of shrimpers out on the horizon where crystal blue sky met dusky water. I was a millionaire. A millionaire without my partner.

I walked on, following the looping path I had worn in the sand.

My new plan called for a changed life. Wanting heat and light, I had scoured the Florida area for property. I wanted a place that would combine business and living areas, since I had always worked from home, but I found nothing suitable. Property of any kind is hard to find in the massive population of southern Florida. The hurricane issue frightened me as well.

The next step was to explore southern Texas. I was somewhat familiar with the area because Mary and I had once vacationed at South Padre Island and fallen in love with the place. I worried that its rural nature would never support a reading room-café combination, but decided I just didn't care. I wanted to live near the water surrounded by what was left of Mary.

Finding the property next to the Port Isabel Lighthouse in Lighthouse Square had been a real stroke of luck. Ruetta Torres, the elderly proprietor of a huge gift shop, had been letting her business go to care for her terminally ill husband. I contacted her realtor, Maddy Henchen, looking for business frontage, just two days after Ruetta finalized her decision to sell.

That same day, I received an e-mail from Maddy, and we both decided it was simply meant to be. Ruetta sold the gift store stock to another business owner, and I bought the huge, empty store with rudimentary living quarters in the back. I hadn't seen it yet, only in photographs provided by Maddy, but the space seemed different enough from my previous home to provide the change I sought.

I looked at my phone to check the time, and then glanced toward the car. I sighed, knowing Oscar Marie would give me grief for leaving her so long in this unfamiliar place. Plus, I had arranged to meet Maddy at the store for a tour of the property and to get the keys, and it was almost time.

Reluctant to leave the solitude of the beach and my rambling thoughts, I turned and walked back to my car and to my new life at Lighthouse Square.

ANGIE

"So anyway, I turned to go through the dining room and that's when Hasty dumped me on her."

Melvin laughed and took another huge bite of pizza. "I'm just glad to have it at all, late or not," he said, his voice almost obliterated by the large bolus of food. Obviously, his mama had never taught him it was impolite to talk with his mouth full. "I was starvin'."

We sat behind the South Padre Island Conference Centre, perched on a concrete wall. The architect hired by the city of

South Padre to design the new center had been a master of his art. The curved design of the building and environs made it feel as though the ocean and building were one. On the back side, where we rested, huge concrete abutments mimicked the arced wings of a gull, and the actual wall on which we sat bowed all the way toward the bay in a graceful slide of smooth, white concrete. On the bay side of the island, where the walls fetched up, the water was quieter and the wildlife active in the shallows.

I knew that from the front, the extensive footprint of the center was low in profile and appeared much smaller than its actual size. Inside, the large convention center boasted forty-five thousand square feet of meeting space, including smaller rooms and an expansive exhibit hall.

One front wall, bearing the huge, colorful mural *Orcas off the Gulf of Mexico* painted in 1994 by artist Robert Wyland, seemed to shout the structure's importance on a global scale. This whaling wall, number fifty-three of the one hundred whaling walls painted by Wyland, featured sea creatures from killer whales to flying fish. It also featured several tarpon, the signature fish for South Padre Island. One of my favorite downtime activities was to study the wall seeking fish the artist had hidden behind outcroppings of rock and seaweed.

The entire bright yellow and cobalt center appeared sleek and modern, and *was* modern with state-of-the-art media equipment in its half dozen conference spaces.

On one side stretched a huge parking lot that sloped toward the water while the other side offered a birding and nature center with wooden walkways spanning marshland and shoreline rich with island flora and fauna.

Another of my favorite pastimes was losing myself for hours in the wildlife area. I would go often during the off-season, the high heat of summer, when I would have the preserve to myself. Ally, the resident alligator, and I had become fast friends. I would share all the peccadilloes of my life while she basked on the shoreline or in the marsh grass, listening with endless patience.

Mama never missed the chicken cubes I filched from the walk-in either. I believe all therapists should be paid, one way or another.

It was peaceful here on the back terrace, with gulls circling lazily overhead and the sun brightened blue of the bay soothing my senses. I reclined back against the wall, my legs and arms dangling comically over both sides, and listened as Melvin chewed.

I thought about my sad woman. I envisioned our romance, our life together as a couple. Was she as fun-loving as me? Would she adore Mama and eagerly become part of our little family? Would I love her family? I wondered if she had a father. I never had and was insatiably curious about all father and daughter relationships.

"So who is she?" Melvin asked, swiping at his mouth with a balled-up napkin.

"Just my future wife." I felt his eyes on me. "Oh, give it up, Mel. You know damn good and well how I am. Don't give me any crap," I muttered, laying a forearm across my eyes.

"Yeah, I get all that, but how can you be *sure* she feels the same way?"

I envisioned the heavy scowl of confusion that no doubt rested on his dark, mustachioed face. I ignored the question, as usual. There was no explanation. You'd think these people, who had known me the whole of my life, would understand that by now.

"I wish I knew her name. She's beautiful. A natural blonde, like me, but way pretty."

"If she's your future wife, where is she?" Melvin asked pointedly. "Is she even here for good or is she just a Winter Texan?"

I chewed my bottom lip, relishing the late afternoon sun on my face. "Now that's a good question. Trust you to bring it up."

Melvin laughed. We'd been friends since primary school. He was one of the few who didn't fear me or scorn me. In fact, he was one of only three people who would stand up to me and shove me back on the reality track when I veered south of it.

"I don't know. I was washing up, so I watched her from the bathroom window when she got in her car and left. Texas tags. She looked so cute carrying her big to-go bag." I smiled at the memory.

Melvin sighed. "Man, you got it bad. I've never seen you like this."

"I've never felt like this," I replied, swinging my legs over and sitting up. "Guess I'm finally in love."

I studied my worn athletic shoes, thinking about the impact this would have on my life. Was I up for the emotional involvement, for the extreme caring that being in love required? Could I expose myself to someone new and let them know how truly strange I really am?

A glob of dried mozzarella clung to one of my shoes. Seeing it reminded me of the day's fiasco and I cringed. I used the toe of the other sneaker to push the crusty cheese off onto the sidewalk. It rested there, shaped curiously, as if eyeing me with disbelief.

"What about Cathy?" Melvin asked. He picked green pepper slices off the pie and munched them like candy.

"We've been done for months. Why?"

"She still has it for you. And you can't tell me you don't know that."

I nodded slowly. Cathy was certainly wonderful enough, and our years together had been pleasant. I'd woken one morning, however, and felt her next to me. Really felt her on that deeper level. I realized I was using her, and she was using me. I had been going for a type of acceptance because being with her pulled me into her small network of island lesbians, a somewhat normal place where I wanted to belong. Cathy's life with me provided financial help and allowed her to be part of the sick sort of fame I possessed here.

"You know, we never made love after that first month. I mean hardly ever. It just wasn't important to her. All the passion went away, I guess. On her part." I stood and straightened my shorts. They had bunched up while I wriggled on the concrete wall.

Melvin tossed a half-eaten slice of green pepper into the box with a huge show of disgust. "Way too much info, Ange."

I laughed at his expression, determined to give him a hard time. "This one though, I can tell, we're gonna be so hot together." I licked my lips and lifted my eyebrows suggestively.

"Okay, lunch is over," Melvin said, closing the pizza box and moving with unusual speed. He lifted his bottle of soda and moved toward the back entrance of the convention center.

I laughed and leapt to grab his arm. "Hey, you gotta pay me for that! Tip me good too, so I can take my new lady love out on the town."

Melvin groaned but managed to juggle pizza box and bottle and fish out his money clip at the same time. He made as if he wasn't going to tip me, just handing over cash for the pie, but ended up laying a ten on me. He winked. I leaned to kiss the end of his nose.

"Later, dude," I said as I headed around the building, shoving the cash into the front pocket of my shorts.

GREY

Maddy Henchen was much smaller than she sounded on the phone. I towered over her at my five-foot-eight height and probably outweighed her by twenty-five pounds. I had expected her to be in her sixties, but certainly not as energetic and perky as she appeared. It seemed her powder blue track suit and white athletic shoes were not just a fashion statement.

After exchanging pleasantries while Maddy unlocked the door, I stepped inside, placed Oscar Marie's carrier in the middle of the large, bare room, and let my gaze roam the building I had bought on faith just a few short months ago. Sound carried under the long, low ceiling, and stepping on the wooden floorboards set off a flurry of echoes.

"This was built in the early 1980s," she explained, laying her hand against the painted cinderblock wall with something like fondness. She turned to look at me. "What do you think of the shelves? Don't they look great?"

I studied the walls laddered with new bookshelves with a critical eye. A young local man named Heriberto had built them and he'd done a good job. They looked like part of the original architecture. I'd been worried, having never met the man, because I usually like to look someone in the eye when I hire them to do a job. Maddy had recommended him and handled the hiring. I could not fault her judgment. I was reminded anew that there was a noticeable difference in something lovingly handmade and something haphazardly produced.

"Yes, he does do good work. You were right," I said, running a hand over the dark, smooth surface of one of the shelves. Mounted on an intricate wooden framework, they stretched the entire length of the walls on both sides, and gleamed in the subdued sunlight from the front windows. "This building is really long, isn't it? Unusual," I murmured.

Oscar Marie mewed as if in agreement.

Maddy slowly blinked her pale blue eyes. "Oh, not an accident. The design allows you to take advantage of the street storefront as well as the Laguna Madre out back. Let me show you."

I followed her toward the back of the building. The northern wall was painted an unusual muted sea-green shade. Strangely attractive. Our target was an age darkened but ornate wooden door on the left side of this wall. I assumed it would guide us into the rear of the store and the living area that Maddy had described on the phone.

"What's this door here?" I paused. A heavy, mysterious looking set of double wooden doors centered in a wall on the right seemed to mock my new ownership.

"Oh, goodness, I almost forgot." Maddy strode to the door on the right and twisted the knob. The door clicked open reluctantly.

"This is a storage area that they used when it was a gift shop. I always thought that the Torreses should have extended their living area into this space. There's even an outside entrance. I guess she didn't want the bother at first, then when Elizondo went into the hospital, she just lost interest," Maddy mused.

I stepped into a large, open room almost as large as the showroom, which contained several wooden carousels that had obviously been used in the gift shop, as well as a few long tables and other random pieces of furniture. Large bare side windows revealed the brightly painted blue cinderblock wall of the business next door. The front facing windows gave me a good view of the huge white cylinder of the Port Isabel Lighthouse.

"Nice," I sighed. "Maybe I could put several sitting rooms in here." I suddenly realized my furniture needs had just leapt up a notch.

"Hmm. Good idea. That would work," Maddy said, a finger to her chin as she considered the space. That same finger then indicated a space just left of the entry. "A little conversation area would be nice here."

"It is going to be a reading room," I murmured. "No reason not to expand into this part."

"Oh, yes. With floor lamps and plump little chairs," Maddy continued her earlier thought. "That would be perfect. There's no place in The Point exactly like that so it would definitely be innovative."

We moved out of that room and into the partially furnished rear apartment. The living area was as small as she had stated, but it was plenty big enough for me. A modest living room, furnished with an overstuffed sofa and one Queen Anne chair, both in desert hues, stood to the left. The bay side of the room offered a dominant dining room bordered by large windows framed by dark beige drapes. This area would be a perfect workroom. I felt the first tentative stirrings of excitement. Maybe the move would be the positive step I needed after all.

I wandered the room as I envisioned how I would set up my worktable. I decided to move the small dining table and chairs to one side, the kitchen side, and set up my drafting table on the northwestern side, sideways to the window so I could look out at the bay as I worked. The view of the bay's slowly rocking water was soothing.

"This room gets plenty of light, and if you open the windows, you'll get some fresh ocean breezes," Maddy said, indicating the windows with the clipboard she held. Her words broke into my creative thoughts. I tried to concentrate on what she was saying. "Sometimes it gets pretty hot, but the wind really helps."

"Yes, this will be a perfect work space for me...the light... perfect."

"That's right, you're a cartoonist. I saw your strip in *Business Weekly* last week. That Sassy Suzy, she gets into the biggest scrapes. When she told Mister Marks that his toast was burnt and he thought she was making fun of his sandals...well, I laughed so hard. I just had to show it to Ernest. You haven't met Ernie yet, he's my husband. He laughed too. We were both wiping our eyes, it was so funny."

I smiled and moved into the small galley-style kitchen. "I'm glad to hear that. The editor really liked that one too. He e-mailed me about it, which is kind of unusual as I usually don't hear from the papers that carry my work."

I switched on the faucet to check the water pressure.

"So you are syndicated? That's wonderful." She cocked her head to one side, her gray wispy hair shifting and waving somewhat companionably. "You're young for that. How did you get into cartooning?"

I opened the refrigerator and thumbed up the cooling fan before answering the same question I'd been asked a million times before. "In college. Although I'd always doodled as a kid." I shrugged. "Guess it's what I'm supposed to do."

Silence grew in the small room. Maddy continued to study me. I sensed her mind clicking like a busy abacus.

"When you called, you said you wanted to open a bookstore and were looking for retail property. What's that about? Are you still going to do Sassy Suzy?" she asked.

"Oh, yes, of course I will." I felt a sudden lurch of alarm. How could I talk about this, about Mary, so soon? Though I lived my life as an openly lesbian cartoonist, I was always a little hesitant to tell strangers anything about my personal life. I decided now was as good a time as any to talk to Maddy.

"My partner, Mary, died a few months ago, and she left me a large collection of books." I said finally, hoping my pain remained hidden. "And I don't really want to sell them, so it's not really a bookstore. It's more of a reading room, coffee shop-type place."

Maddy grunted slightly. Her eyes widened. "Ah, I see, and it's a good idea. I am so sorry for your loss, though."

"Thank you," I said.

I saw the questions forming. People always wanted to know how she died—assuming, by my young age, that it was cancer or perhaps a car accident. I had no easy answers I wanted to share so, turning my attention back to the kitchen, I effectively dismissed her interest and forestalled any further queries.

"Wow, would you look at this," I said, peering through the large window over the sink. I pulled open the kitchen door, which led onto a wide, square deck with a private dock that stretched a good half mile into the bay. It was a breathtaking scene, and I suddenly, completely understood the high listing price of the mostly nondescript property.

"Isn't it wonderful?" Maddy sighed next to me. "I remember when Ruetta built this place. Her husband, Elizondo, was in a wheelchair by then, and she used to bring him out here while she minded the shop. All of his retired buddies would stop by and visit with him, and there'd be a regular *pachanga* going on back here."

"*Pachanga?*"

She laughed and explained. "South Texas barbeque party. Huge."

The bay appeared calm, but that was just an illusion. Hundreds of birds, pelicans, and gulls mostly, moved busily about the raised dock feeding and basking in the fierce sunlight. The rocky shoreline teemed with smaller birds. Beneath the boards of the dock, dunlins and egrets chased after hermit crabs and large, glossy water gliders. From everywhere came the sounds of birds calling directions to one another, waves slapping the sand and rocks with gleeful abandon, and the wind baying mournfully through the deck railings.

"Oh, my heavens," I muttered. "You said waterfront but I had no idea. I'll never get any work done."

Maddy laughed at my dilemma. "Right enough. When Ernest and I used to come here from the north as Winter Texans, I always brought some project I thought I'd get done during the winter, like needlepoint or quilting. I've got to admit though, I'd spend days just watching the water and in March, back home I'd go, that unfinished project going right back with me."

"I sure hope that doesn't really happen to me," I said, leading the way back to the kitchen and firmly closing the door.

"You'll be living here, like we do now," Maddy counseled. "You do sort of get used to it after a while."

"Oh, so you live here full time now. I should have guessed since you're working here."

We moved into the relative dimness of the living room. Maddy indicated that I should take a seat on the sofa.

"I do, and I certainly get more done these days after living in Port Isabel for the past three years. And speaking of getting things done, let's get this last bit of paperwork out of the way so you can get on with moving yourself and settling in. When is the truck coming?"

She handed me the clipboard, and I began signing the viewing papers. I'd signed and had notarized the sale papers a month or so ago, but these papers had to do with Maddy's real estate company. "The books will be here in about three hours. I sold everything else."

"Everything?"

I heard the disbelief in her voice. "Pretty much. There's a new bed on the truck, but I auctioned off the contents of the house before I sold it. The SUV is full of some stuff too."

"Ah, I see. Listen, do you need some help here?" Maddy asked as I signed.

"How do you mean? Unpacking?" I answered absently, reading the mostly meaningless small print.

"That, or like getting the store ready, or minding it while you draw. I know several young men who would be happy to help out."

I looked at her when I handed the clipboard back. Had I noted a subtle emphasis on men? I had to chuckle just a little. I guess Grey Graham would be an interesting new topic of conversation in Port Isabel before the end of the day.

"Hmm, a good idea. I have your card and will maybe give you a call after I get settled in."

Maddy smiled and started to respond, but a loud voice echoing in the front of the building arrested her.

"Yo, Maddy, where ya at?" The gruff voice was accompanied by loud staccato barking and Oscar Marie's angry squalls.

I leapt to my feet and raced into the front. A balding, heavyset man stood next to Oscar Marie's carrier. He held the leads of three small dogs. The Lhasa apso and two fox terriers were digging at the metal grate on the front of the carrier.

"Holy shit!" the man exclaimed. "Someone left a damned cat out here." He pulled the dogs away from the carrier. "Hish now! Y'all boys just move on back here now."

Poor Oscar Marie. Her thick black fur had bristled into a broad mane by the time I reached her carrier. Her large topaz eyes were darkened by fear. She stared at me accusingly.

"It's okay, baby," I crooned, wishing I could open the cage and hold her. I knew better, though. She would take off like a ruptured balloon and the chase would be on. I satisfied myself by moving the crate around, thereby blocking her view of the dogs with the solid side of it, hoping to calm her.

"I am so sorry, ma'am," the man said, securely shortening the dogs' leads. "I was blinded by the sun when I stepped in, and they were on her before I knew what was afoot."

I looked into his sorrowful brown eyes and knew his apology was heartfelt. "That's okay. No harm done."

"Ms. Graham, this is Ernie, my husband," Maddy said. "Ernie, this is cartoonist Grey Graham, our newest Point resident."

"Well, pleased to meet you, Ms. Graham," Ernie said, extending his hand. He indicated the dogs. "These miscreants are Buffy, JJ and Diablo."

"But we call him Dabbles most of the time," Maddy interjected, lifting the tan and white terrier up for snuggles. "He's not such a devil anymore," she added in a crooning singsong. Dabbles responded by lovingly licking her nose with his long pink tongue.

"You do spoil him rotten, Mad," Ernie said, shaking his head and smiling indulgently.

Maddy grimaced at me. "They're our kids," she explained.

I held up a staying palm and nodded. "No need to tell me about it. I feel the same about my Oscar Marie."

Maddy lowered Dabbles to the floor and took the lead from her husband. "We do apologize for the fright. Will she be okay?"

I smiled to reassure her. "She's a Maine Coon breed and tough as nails. She just wants out of this carrier so she can explore her new home."

"I bet. Well, there's plenty to explore here. This old building has nooks and crannies galore."

"Elizondo sure loved this old place," Ernie added, his voice echoing boldly in the open space. He turned to his wife. "Did you show her the deck out back?"

"Now, Ernest, why do you think I'm even here?" she said archly. "Of course I did. And she loved it as much as we do, I'm sure."

She glanced at me for support and I hastily agreed.

"Well, dear, here are your keys, both sets. The red dot is the front door, green is the side door, and blue is for the back door. If you have any questions or problems, don't you hesitate to give me a call."

I felt a sudden urge to ask them to stay, to have dinner, a glass of wine, but knew the idea was ridiculous. I didn't know them. Beyond that, I wasn't even settled in yet, and was certainly not ready to entertain. I guess starting anew on a life alone was proving more daunting than I had expected.

"Thank you so much," I said instead. "For everything. You have been just wonderful."

"My pleasure, child, and again, I'm sorry for your loss. I hope over time you will come to love The Point—your new home—as much as we have."

I leaned forward and drew her into a brief hug with hated tears welling in my eyes. "I'm sure I will," I said, even as an unfamiliar loneliness raged in my heart.

ANGIE

The nature preserve beckoned enticingly on my right, but I had other plans. I guided my open Jeep along Beach Road, all the way off South Padre and over the Queen Isabella Causeway, the stiff ocean wind actually buffeting me around on my worn leather driver's seat. I passed Lighthouse Square quickly, praying for a green light in case Mama was looking out the front windows of The Fat Mother.

Within minutes, I was at a low, nondescript building that faced seaward on one of the many finger inlets of Laguna Madre, just off the main highway in Port Isabel, a few blocks from the restaurant. I parked my Jeep and took a minute to let the powerful ocean wind caress my face and play in my hair. I tilted my face toward the sun. Responsibilities nagged at me. I knew Mama would need me for dinner setups, but this felt just so darn good. I guess I am a hedonist at heart, enjoying my own outdoor creature comforts.

Sighing reluctantly, I leapt from the Jeep and raced up to the heavy metal double doors of the building. A small bas-relief metal sign posted on the wall by the door declared it the Wilson Special School. As usual, I slapped the sign gently as I passed through the unlocked right side.

It had taken us a long time and a ton of begging to get Captain Petey Wilson to part with the startup and rent money for this facility, the South Padre Island Center for Extraordinary Youth, or Wilson's SPICEY as the residents referred to it. The building had been a church originally, and had passed into the hands of the Port Isabel Town Council when the congregation moved inland to Bayview.

A gentle wave of sound hit me as I veered left of the main activity room and entered my cubbyhole of an office. A hand-lettered sign on the door proclaimed it as Angie's office. The letters were misaligned and the spelling off, but I adored it nevertheless.

The boy who had drawn the placard, David Imuss, had asphyxiated in his sleep one night about a year ago. I'd been heartbroken, but the sign he'd made for me helped keep his memory alive. We'd had a lot of good times together.

I sighed and checked my desk for messages. No news was good news. I smiled. My position at the school as teacher slash activities director gobbled up time like a corporate Pac-Man. I dropped into the squealing desk chair and opened the lower right-hand drawer. I lifted out the cashbox and unlocked it, using a key kept on my car key lanyard. Separating out the ten dollars tip from the restaurant money for Melvin's pizza, I slid it into the cashbox, then re-locked it securely. My stash was growing. It was up to four hundred eighty dollars, just from tips and two odd jobs during the past two weeks.

I let the office door drift closed behind me as I strode into the main hall. Stretching a good forty feet in each direction, the hall provided plenty of room for the various wheelchairs and mobility equipment needed by our kids. Today, they were finishing up the art project I had laid out on the class schedule, making castles from clay, and then drawing them. It had also been a history lesson about the Middle Ages.

Connie and Emilio, two of the older kids, were signing vigorously at the end of the table. I watched long enough to realize it was a dirty joke before I looked away, embarrassed. Maria, bless her heart, sat alone as usual, but alert and ready to help if asked.

Maria's case really kept me in a low state of unease. Raped and beaten as a young teen, her face slashed, she was now twenty-one and had little life beyond her home and these school walls. A couple of years ago, I had taken her out once for smoothies, just the two of us. Although she'd been amenable to the outing, she'd quickly become a bundle of nerves and tightly held fear when a group of loud, rowdy boys entered the diner. It would take a long time for those psychological scars to heal, which saddened me.

Upon seeing me, Sally and Tommy came loping over, and as usual, I squeezed them in a huge hug until they laughed and pushed away.

"Angie, is it Monday?" Tommy asked, his round face screwing up in a thoughtful moue.

"Nope, just passing through. It's almost time for you guys to go home anyway," I replied, taking Tommy's hand and pulling him along. I reached for Sally's, but she was experiencing a fit of jealousy and pulled away. I lurched to one side and grabbed the eight-year-old around her chubby waist, lifting her easily. That caused a harsh bark of laughter and diminishing giggles from her. I pulled Tommy along and carried Sally like a sack of potatoes as

I approached Melissa who stood with her arms folded across her chest, watching my antics with a stern frown.

"Hey, 'Lissa," I said, amused by her obvious disapproval.

"Now, Angie," she began, freeing Sally and placing her feet back on the floor. "You know we do not manhandle the children."

Melissa Godwin, as her name subtly implied, was God's messenger to the world. Speaking in a soft but firm southern drawl, her word was law. I often brazenly flew in the face of that godliness. We had a good working relationship, nevertheless, not that it mattered so much. She taught and handled everything at the center on the days I helped Mama at the restaurant, and I worked here on her church volunteer days.

Sally sidled next to me and insinuated her little hand into mine, as if signifying her approval of our play. I squeezed her hand gently, eliciting a new giggle. Tommy wandered back to the activities table.

Melissa pursed her lips. "Why are you here today?" she asked.

"Just checking in. I was in the neighborhood."

"Well, that woman from the courthouse called again this morning. I don't know *what* to tell her," she added emphatically.

I groaned inwardly. I should have known. Just because it wasn't written in a phone memo didn't mean there was no bad news.

Two weeks ago, snooty Frankee Howell had come by with her camera and her following of good old boy lackeys. Seems the Port Isabel Town Council had decided that SPICEY, a mere medical open enrollment charter, wasn't nearly as important as the proposed Port Isabel Marina that would span all three undeveloped fingers of land where they stretched into the bay. Unfortunately, as owners of the property, the town council had every right to raze the old, creaky building and replace it with the slick, ultra-modern clubhouse they'd shown me in their artist renderings. They wanted us out as quickly as possible.

"There is nothing to tell her, 'Lissa. We're not closing until we find a better location."

Melissa eyed me worriedly, so I apologetically released Sally's hand and scooted her toward the clay piled next to her abandoned chair. Nervously, I moved to the table and began neatening the craft items, eventually lining up crayons by color.

"Angie, honey, they are bound and determined to make this part of the new marina. This old building is going away. The sooner you realize that, the better."

I tried soothing my emotions by placing crayons in perfect rows, by size now as well as by color. I did not look at her. "And where are the kids supposed to go?" I countered angrily. "We can't afford anywhere else."

Melissa didn't answer right away. A strained silence fell between us. Emma Rachel, Melissa's thirty-something daughter, approached.

"Mother, it's time for Frederick's therapy so he can go home," she said softly.

I looked at her and saw the concern shining in her dark blue eyes. A gentle soul, Emma hated any kind of confrontation. I smiled widely to put her mind at ease and strode toward Frederick's bed.

Gabby, his private nurse, struggled to force the moveable hospital bed back to its original flat position. I helped her with the lever and soon Fred lay supine. Gabby checked his maze of tubing to make sure no tubes had kinked. I propped a hip up on the bed next to the little guy.

"Hey, handsome, what's up with you today? You doing all right?" I leaned close so his eyes could focus. He had nystagmus, so his eyes fluttered constantly. It was a little disconcerting, but I was used to it. I chucked him under the chin. His loopy grin made me laugh. "Good. Glad to hear that. Therapy time. You ready?"

I adjusted his bib and helped Gabby straighten his legs. I moved back to the head of the bed and spoke to him. "I gotta run back to help Mama now, but you just holler out if any of these women give you a hard time, you hear? I got Maria watching your back and she'll tell me if they don't treat you right."

Frederick squirmed with pleasure and emitted chuckling sounds. Maria was one of his favorite friends at SPICEY. I gently pulled his gnarled hands apart and pressed his stiff arms toward the bed, patting his hands to reassure him.

Gabby worked on his legs. I watched her as I placed Fred's wheelchair close to the bed and locked the wheels, noting anew how capable and powerful her movements were. She was amazing. Frederick's cerebral palsy had pulled his limbs and torso into tight bows, and he needed therapy twice daily to prevent the contractures from becoming worse.

It wasn't an easy job. Gabby might have weighed a hundred pounds sopping wet so it was hard going. Thankfully, though Freddy was fifteen, he was small for his age. I admired her determined Latin features and glossy black hair as she used her slight body weight to lengthen, and then flex Fred's limbs. Little beads of sweat popped out on her forehead. I mentally chided myself for my unseemly interest. Gabby had a handsome husband and two young boys at home.

I turned away and waved farewell to the group. At the door, I paused and looked back.

Almost the entire group was in attendance today. I noted that twelve-year-old Delicia Gonzales seemed down, and I regretted I couldn't take the time to go talk to her. Someone, probably Emma Rachel, had situated her pillows properly so she sat upright in her wheelchair, but she didn't seem interested in the school project or the cleanup. Her small hands rested in her lap and her gaze was vacant.

Tommy and Sally, both Down Syndrome children, more than made up for Delicia's disinterest by chasing one another around the table. Tommy threatened Sally with a wet lump of clay. I sighed, knowing the situation would end badly.

I glanced at my watch. Father Sephria would arrive within the hour to help Melissa and Emma Rachel load the children into the van. I was glad to see that Connie and Emilio, my more mobile teenagers, were behaving themselves now and helping with cleanup. Sadness filled me when I turned to leave. Where would they all go when the town council evicted us?

GREY

I loved my new home and had enjoyed a peaceful, restful night lulled by the sound of the waves slapping the shore, since the sole window in the bedroom overlooked the bay.

My small, cozy room with its newly carpeted floor and fresh paint on the walls was down a short hall from the living room. The apartment bathroom with a huge walk-in shower—no doubt configured for Mr. Torres' special needs—was just off the bedroom. Space was tight. My queen-sized bed barely fit, but overall the room was womblike and comforting.

I wasn't quite sure where my clothing would go as there

was no closet and certainly no room for a bureau. I studied the room, seeking inspiration, but finally shrugged and carried my empty coffee cup back to the kitchen. I would deal with that issue later.

I took my coffee with me out onto my private boardwalk after I made a second cup. I hadn't bothered to dress because my pajama shorts and T-shirt were more than adequate to brave the heated breezes from the west.

The Laguna Madre, that peaceful expanse of sequestered ocean, stretched as far as the eye could see. Waves waltzed for me, sparkling in the bright morning sunlight. I felt a sense of peace steal over me and suddenly realized that muscles that had been clenched since Mary's death had began to loosen at last.

I dropped my gaze to a young pelican below me. He was hunched on a low piling, seemingly reluctant to greet the new day. As if cheering him on, the growing sunlight forced warmth into his mass of tan feathers.

As I watched him, I took a long mental health inventory and realized that I would always miss Mary. Her loss was a grief that would stay with me forever. My task now was to learn to deal with the pain and find a way to bury it deeply so it wouldn't tug at me day after day as it had since I learned of the explosion. I could do this. I had to. It was my only salvation.

The pelican peered up at me with one eye, his ungainly features manifesting curiosity. I smiled at him, wishing I had bread to share. He stirred and looked away, his feathers rippling. Realizing that I might be intruding on his morning routine, I turned and headed back to the building.

Approaching my new home from the bay side, I noted again how powerful the structure seemed. The long, low building was made of concrete and rebar to withstand the storms sprouting seaward. The huge white cylinder and black lamp platform of the Port Isabel Lighthouse towered behind it like an art deco church steeple. A short chain of other cinderblock businesses stretched to the left, but I was surprised to note that mine was the only one with a usable dock. The other businesses backed onto scrub grass that sloped down into the rocky tidal basin.

To my immediate right was an access road that led to a tall network of condominiums that had been built on a perilous looking outcropping of land. Beyond that, on the other side of the road, was a cemetery with an ornate wrought-iron fence surrounding it. I made a mental note to check that out as soon as possible.

I could just see the northern end of the line of restaurants and gift shops that also faced the lighthouse, but at a ninety degree angle from my place. The one on the far end, The Fat Mother, had been quite an adventure my first afternoon in Port Isabel. I thought of the family who owned the place and had to smile. I made a mental note to find a good dry cleaner so I could salvage the shirt I'd worn on my first day in town.

Bringing my attention back to my building, I found myself squinting my eyes and studying it. If you looked at it just so from this angle, it looked like any small beachside home with extensive decking and large windows.

The small kitchen was situated so that it was filled with sunlight just about all day. I had already filled the windowsills and window shelves left by Ruetta with my collection of colored glass bottles in varying shapes. The bottles winked at me in a rainbow of primary colored joy as I approached. I had also hung wind chimes along the outside eaves. They now sang a cheery welcome.

I shook my head, scoffing at what now made home for me, wind chimes and bottles, while the rest of my new abode was in shambles with full packing boxes littering the floors.

The book area wasn't much better. The large, open space was bisected by crates of Mary's books. I suppose the intimidating task of unpacking kept me dallying out here in the wind and sun. I looked back at the water and sighed. The heat of the rising day caressed my cheeks and eyes. Maybe that wasn't the only thing keeping me out here.

I entered the bright kitchen with new resolve. I would get the unpacking started, at least.

After a quick shower, I threw on a pair of loose cotton shorts and a T-shirt, and set about tackling the crates of books. When packing them at the house, I had divided them as Mary had, by category, and then subdivided by author. This method had manifested into more than a hundred small boxes in four dozen crates.

I stood staring at the file stretching the length of the bookstore and sighed. Where to begin? I looked around at the walls filled with empty bookshelves gleaming greedily in the early morning sunlight that snuck in through the front windows.

I popped open the first crate and crouched down. Turning the first box so I could read the label, I saw it was *Favorites*. These books had been kept closest to Mary in the overcrowded library, on a makeshift shelf above her old wooden desk.

Pain seared through me at the thought of seeing them again. I almost pushed the box aside. I reconsidered, missing her fiercely, so I jerked the box open, freeing a waft of ancient perfume. Mary used to tell me that books were real to her because they absorbed the lives of the people who had loved them. I could almost sense that now. I guess living with her so long had given me some appreciation for the bound word after all.

I lifted out an armful of books and carried them to the small shelves recessed next to the main desk and the first coffee bar. I placed them upright by size, my hand lingering on each one. I thought of Mary's hands on these same books which, of course, led to thoughts of Mary's hands on me. I pushed the memories away. Falling into mournful reminiscences would not help me get through the day. I had advertised a grand opening in two weeks and simply had to have everything in place by then.

Going back for a second armload, I was able to awkwardly drag the mostly empty crate over to the coffee area. I turned to place the books on the shelf and stopped in my tracks. A book which, just moments before, had been standing with the others, now lay open on the shelf in front of the vertical rank. I stared at it, wondering how I had managed to pull it into such a perfect position when I turned away. Laughing at my heretofore unknown sleight of hand, I gathered up the book and slid it into the waiting slot it had occupied earlier. I felt a weird sense of unease when I turned away.

Emptying the box, I stood back and studied the section of shelving. My first filled shelf. I wondered whether a cell phone photo was warranted. Maybe I would put it on my recently neglected Facebook page to prove to my friends that I would be okay.

I needed to share this moment with them. I fished the phone out of my pocket and captured the shelf from several angles. I uploaded the photos to my profile page, then thrust the phone back into my pocket. Sighing, I turned to the next box in the crate.

ANGIE

Sweat tickled my face when it escaped the protective buffer of my eyebrow and wriggled along my cheek. I ducked my head, swabbing the sweat on the shoulder of my T-shirt.

I liked the rhythm of the elliptical and how my thighs bunched and released with every stroke of the flywheel. I glanced over at Cathy, noting how new musculature had developed in her upper arms and shoulders.

"Damn!" I panted. "What's with the new definition? What are you doing that you're not telling me about?"

Cathy looked at me and popped out her earbuds. I heard Bonnie Raitt's plaintive voice emitting faintly through them. "What definition?"

I nodded toward her upper body. "Shoulders." I breathed deeply, trying to get the proper oxygen to my thigh muscles.

"Mostly pull-ups," she answered, panting as much as I was, but she never sweated the way I did. I invariably looked like a drowned rat by the time I left the workout floor, but Cathy always looked fresh as a daisy. Made me furious. Now I could also envy her muscular gain.

"How many?"

She grinned at me. "More than you want to do, sweetie."

I scowled at her and picked up speed.

"How are things with the center?"

I shrugged. "What can I tell you? Frankee is relentless."

Cathy slowed and checked the readings. She nodded as if satisfied and dismounted. Sighing with relief, I followed suit. Moments later, we sat at the juice bar sipping water. I propped a foot on an empty barstool and massaged my calf.

"What are you going to do, Ange?" Cathy asked, watching me.

"I don't know." I glanced at her and an idea exploded in my brain. Cathy saw my smile and recoiled.

"Uh-oh, I know that look."

"Is your uncle still on the planning board?"

Cathy frowned. "You mean Lewis? Yeah, I think he is. What does that have to do..." Her eyes widened.

"You could talk to him." I lowered my leg and turned my full attention on her. "I'm sure he could plead our case."

Worry furrowed her brow. "But would he?" She shook her head. "I don't think so, hon. You know how he is."

"Yeah, but he's always liked me. And what we're doing is so important and so good for the community. Think about Fred. He'd be stuck up in that big house with only Gabby for company. And Frances. Oh, my God, she hovers. The boy can't get in a breath while she's around."

Cathy eyed me with an exasperated expression. "I know how his mom is, Angie, and I know what you do is important, but it's a marina, for God's sake. It's like trying to stop the spinning of the earth." She paused and laid a palm on my sweaty forearm. "We are a tourist-based city. You should know that above all people, with your mama's restaurant."

I fumed inwardly, feeling her hopelessness for a few seconds, and then pulled my arm away. "Just talk to him, Cathy. What could it hurt?" I took a huge swig of water and wiped my mouth with my palm.

Cathy's face took on that pouty look I knew so well. I also knew I'd gotten my way. "Fine. I'll talk to him. He is such an ass, though. I hate having anything to do with him."

She turned petulantly, and her knee pressed against my thigh for a few brief seconds. A wave of images swept across me. I stiffened. It seems that Uncle Lewis had once been way too familiar with a much younger Cathy Lloyd. How had I never picked that up before? Just as I was preparing to tell her to forget it, Cathy's cell phone trilled and she turned away to answer it.

Some people called what I had a gift from God. I didn't see it that way. I plucked at my T-shirt, trying to get some air beneath it to cool my sweaty body. The so-called gift never brought me much more than a lot of fancy footwork trying to explain myself.

There's a good deal of B.S. in the mainstream media about how being psychic could help people, protect them from harm. It's been my experience that the flashes usually come too late to do any good. I guess it could be useful after the fact. I had helped out the Los Fresnos Police Department a couple of times, looking for lost people and where bodies could be found. And like one of the bodies, floating bloated and discolored in a resaca near Blackfoot Drive, the images that came unbidden to me about people's personal lives could be just as disturbing.

"It's Nancy," Cathy said. "She wants me to come over and watch the kids while she takes Eddie to the doctor."

I was alarmed. Eddie was the youngest of Cathy's sister's four children and had been sickly since birth. "What's wrong with Eddie?"

Cathy held up a calming hand. "Just a well visit, Ange. Nothing to get worked up about. He's actually been doing pretty good, gaining weight even."

I sighed with relief. "Oh, I'm glad. So you're going over there?"

"Yeah, wanna come help?"

I shook my head. "Gotta work at the center all afternoon."

Cathy rose. "Well, let's go shower. Good workout, huh?"

I hesitated. "Listen, you go ahead. I want to stretch out this calf."

Cathy studied me. I knew she knew I still wasn't comfortable being naked with her. A small glint of victory shone in her dark eyes, which angered me. I hated that she still thought she was irresistible to me. Cathy really believed it, and she also believed that, although it was certainly over between us, I'd be hard pressed not to take advantage if she offered. As if.

I leaned back and smiled at her, determined to knock her down a notch. "Besides, I just saw Steph go into the locker room. You better jump on that. You know she has the hots for you."

Cathy swiveled her head toward the locker rooms. "How do you know that?" she asked eagerly.

"Trust me," I intoned importantly. Actually, I was fishing, but beautiful Stephanie Rutherford had recently broken up with her longtime girlfriend, Molly. It wasn't hard imagining Cathy and Steph hooking up.

Cathy glanced at me and frowned before she walked toward the locker rooms.

I wondered what she was thinking. Sometimes I wish my so-called gift worked across long distances.

GREY

The books were unpacked at last, surprising because I'd had to pause and deal with several business phone calls during the morning as well. All the books were not placed perfectly yet, but at least the packing crates were empty and stacked in a corner near the front door. The local branch of the trucking company I had used would pick them up the following day.

I rested my forearms on the long coffee counter in the back and studied the space. I was pleased. It was large and wide open, but I had made it cozier by trundling in and utilizing some of the antique wooden displays from the side storeroom. They provided interesting focal points down each side of the room as well. Some of the larger, educational books had found a nice perch there and their covers intrigued me.

I had shelved the books in the categories Mary had set for them and placed handwritten labels on each of the shelves. I would print more permanent ones on the computer before opening day. I grabbed my phone and made a note to pick up shelf placards on my next trip into Harlingen or Brownsville.

I also began counting. Altogether, I planned to set up six conversation areas in the main room and three in the storeroom. I studied the room, visualizing as I furiously typed into my phone. I would need about ten floor lamps and a half dozen table lamps. I mentally placed four sofas and a good dozen easy chairs, as well as coffee tables, end tables and accent tables. Plus the two counters flanking the back of the room would each have two Keurig coffeemakers with racks of K-cup possibilities.

I tapped my phone against my chin, still undecided about how the customers would pay for coffee or tea. I knew I had to hire an attendant, at least one, so I needed to pay his or her salary, plus the cost of the beverages and the expensive cups. I envisioned a chalkboard behind each counter, listing the usual costs plus daily specials. That would work. I added them to my list.

I agonized over whether to buy a fancy computerized cash register, but decided to table that issue for now and just keep physical books for a while to see how things went. I did not want to charge a reading fee, never would, because in honor of Mary I wanted to provide her books to everyone, no matter their ability to pay. I realized suddenly that I hadn't thought of her all day. I'd been busy enough to set aside my grief. I sighed.

Checking my Facebook account, I saw that several friends had commented on the pictures I had uploaded earlier that day, some wondering how I'd managed to "shop" in such an effect. Frowning in puzzlement, I called up my mobile uploads and saw the photos.

Not seeing much beyond a shelf of books, I walked to the front of the store closer to the daylight brightening the front windows. I rotated my phone to make the photos larger and that was when I saw what they meant. If you looked at the photo just right, you could see a ghostly hand reaching out to touch the spines of the books. The effect was only in one of the photos, so certainly had to be an errant shaft of sunlight that looked hand-like.

I laughed at the illusion and typed in a joking response even as I stretched my shoulders and neck, deciding I'd had just about enough work for one day. I glanced toward the sky, through the front windows, and saw there was still a good bit of daylight left. With my back and legs cramped from lifting stacks of books, I quickly left the Bookmark and locked up, eager to walk off the stiffness and explore my new home.

The foot traffic in Lighthouse Square had lessened markedly as the day eased into afternoon. Though the parking slots in front of the lighthouse were all filled, I knew the passengers were likely settling in at the string of restaurants surrounding the area.

As it was getting late, I made a beeline for the crosswalk and crossed over the four lanes of highway. After walking two blocks, I came to the mesquite-shaded entrance of the Port Isabel Museum, a place I had read about in a brochure picked up at The Fat Mother.

I passed through a small gift shop and paid seven dollars to enter. As soon as I stepped into the museum proper, I was surrounded by shell artifacts from the 1500s. My interest was piqued as I've always been something of a history buff. I studied the conch shells the natives and early settlers used as hammers and the sharpened shells they used as scrapers and knives. The ingenuity of early man never failed to amaze me. I also saw a fossilized mammoth tooth as big around as my thigh. The thought of a creature that size was daunting.

Settling the lower Rio Grande Valley had been hit or miss for a good while, it seemed. The Spaniards had numerous deadly encounters with the natives. Not until the late 1600s was a successful colony set up near Port Isabel. The next case held photographic and artistic displays about the development of ranches and the establishment of the *vaqueros* or Mexican cowboys.

I was intrigued to see that most of the ranch land in the lower Rio Grande Valley had been granted by Spanish royalty to a select handful of families. These families set up huge cattle ranches throughout the area, including what would become Padre Island. I had no idea the island had been a cattle ranch for so long.

I learned that Texas and Mexico fought for independence from Spain using pirates and smugglers to get valley products to ports such as Corpus Christi and New Orleans. Land disputes led to the Mexican War of 1846 which set the Rio Grande River as the boundary dividing the two nations. I studied lists of soldiers' names and imagined the young, eager faces falling under enemy fire.

I followed the serpentine layout of the museum and chased the history of Point Isabel which became Port Isabel in 1927. I learned about the steamboats on the Rio Grande, transporting cargo north and bringing back goods to the valley. The Civil War placed South Texas in a strategic tug of war that caused it to suffer a good bit of destruction. The 1870s brought the rise of railroad barons and the 1900s saw South Texas dealing with the Mexican Revolution, and later becoming a prime fishing and tourist destination. My head was spinning by the time I finished the last display and stepped out of the coolness, back to the steaming sidewalk of Port Isabel.

I made my way back across Highway 100 and entered the old light keeper's cottage where the Port Isabel Chamber of Commerce had established a tourist bureau. I checked out a few brochures, picked up a detailed history and a phone book, walked across the lawn, mounted the ten or so steps, and walked into the dimness of the lighthouse. Black iron stairs spiraled into the air above me.

"Think I'll make it?" I asked the young college student minding the table just inside the entry.

"I think so," she said with a shrug. "You look pretty fit."

I laughed at her. "Okay. Well, I'll give it a try."

"Just remember to hold onto the railings," she cautioned.

I took one more glance at the cautionary placards, especially the fact that there were almost seventy steps to the top, and began the trek.

By the intermediate landing, I was breathing hard and feeling just a touch claustrophobic. I made it all the way to the supply room level, and up the ladder into the lantern room. From there, the view was breathtaking.

The Queen Isabella bridge stretched into the distance. South Padre Island, with its friendly fat hotel fingers reaching toward the sky, hovered on the horizon like a peaceful daydream. I noted the huge fishing pier that stretched into the bay and the stylized pirate ship moored at the end, and made a mental note to check it out on my next exploratory foray.

Over to my right, I saw a huge smiley face and realized it was a parasail following a speedboat, both small from my vantage point.

I moved to the other side of the lantern room. The town of Port Isabel sprawled before me in all its historic waterfront glory. I saw bristling, needle-masted shrimpers off in the distance, resting at dock in the many little inlets that made up the calm union of land and ocean. I stayed there enjoying the beauty and the movement below until I heard a young couple mounting the stairs beneath me. When they entered the lantern room, I greeted them and made my way carefully back down to terra firma.

I strode down the grassy knoll and let myself into the Bookmark, my mind whirling with the information I now knew about my new home. Port Isabel had a strange and wonderful history, and I was glad I'd chosen to live there.

I bolted the door behind me and reset the alarm. My footsteps echoed as I crossed the floor. I realized anew how glad I would be to fill the remaining floor space with furniture and warmth. As I started to go into the apartment, I paused at the door. Something was different.

I turned and studied the huge room, my heart tapping in my chest. I saw nothing unusual. I moved to open the storeroom door, thinking that I should check there when it hit me.

I whirled around and gasped. Every other bookshelf bore a neat stack of books. They weren't side by side vertically, as I had left them, but stacked horizontally, one atop the other, on the front of the shelf, in front of the other books.

I took a moment to wonder about the oddity of it. Why had someone come in and stacked them on every other shelf? What could be the purpose? Why not each shelf?

I eased my cell phone from my pocket as I walked slowly, carefully, back toward the front door. How had someone bypassed my alarm system? I had even changed the code after moving in so no one, not even Maddy, had that information.

I glanced at the alarm panel, noting that the alarm appeared to be working correctly. I punched in my code and opened the door, glancing back one more time even as my fingers pressed the emergency call button on my phone.

ANGIE

It was just like Frankee to keep me waiting.

I stared grumpily at Amy, who'd been a secretary at the courthouse since we were in high school together. She felt my stare and glanced up apologetically.

"I'm sorry, Ange," she whispered. "She can be such a bitch."

"I know," I mumbled, and sighed. "It's just I'm supposed to be working this morning and instead, I'm here doing this crap."

Amy nodded sympathetically just as the chime on her phone sounded. "Cool! You can go in now," she told me perkily.

I bolted for the door before she had finished her comment. Frankee sat behind her overlarge wooden desk, peering at me from over the top of her small reading glasses.

"In a hurry, are we?" she said sarcastically, removing the glasses and setting them aside.

"Frankee, you have no right to keep me out there for almost a solid hour. I got stuff to do," I fumed.

"I hope packing up is on your to-do list."

My mouth dropped open. "Man, you are one heartless—"

"Now, Angie," She indicated the chair in front of her desk. "I'm not unsympathetic to your plight. I kept you waiting because I was on the phone with several realty companies, trying to find you a new place. No luck yet."

I sat down and leaned forward. "You know we can't afford anyplace else. If not for Captain Petey, we wouldn't have what we have now."

"Don't forget the kindness of the council. We've given your little home school a venue for a measly hundred a month for many years now. I think that's pretty generous. But now we have to take that property back. We need it back."

"But Frankee, why do we even *need* another marina? We've got Charlie's place, the Sea Ranch, the Tarpon, a dozen others!"

Frankee frowned and rolled a pencil back and forth on her desk. "You know as well as I do, Angie, that the Fingers are going to waste. They could be generating all kinds of revenue."

"Are we that poor that we have to dump a bunch of special needs kids out on the street?" I eyed her, willing her to get it.

"That's not fair."

"Neither is what you guys are doing!" I stood and paced across her beautiful red Oriental rug. "I don't have enough to put down on a place and you know what rents run around here." I paused and glared at her. "You are effectively closing my school."

Frankee frowned. "Look, Angie, I may be new to this community, but I understand how close-knit everything is here. But maybe it's time to let it go. You have, what? A master's in education now? You could be a principal in a real school somewhere."

I nodded angrily and dramatically. "True, but that's not what I want. Mama needs me at the restaurant and these kids need me. They need their school."

Frankee stood, dismissing me from her busy schedule. I suddenly realized the futility of our conversation.

"It was voted on, Angie. The building will go April first, after spring break. You have until then," she said calmly. "We'll help you in any way we can, but I'm afraid our decision is made."

***

I couldn't go into The Fat Mother right away so I sat outside in my Jeep. Keen disappointment rested in my stomach like I'd eaten a bag full of rocks. I wasn't real clear on what I had expected from Frankee, maybe a heart, but I now realized how unrealistic any expectation had been.

My mind lit on possibilities like butterflies searching from flower to flower for nectar. My three-room cottage was way too small and not on any main routes. There was a hall that the Elks had used for a while, but it had huge plumbing and sewage problems. The rest of The Point was mostly made up of tourist businesses.

I let my mind roam further out. Los Fresnos had recently abandoned a youth center due to its age and built a brand-new one. It was an old community. Most of the buildings there had issues and were priced high regardless. Bayview had nothing suitable. Brownsville did, but they were way expensive and the kids would have to be transported pretty far. Ditto Harlingen. The island was way out of our reach financially and property was severely limited anyway.

I felt as though my head was going to explode. Even though I tried hard not to, I was getting a bit miffed with the universe. I'm one of those people who believe that all things happen for a reason, a reason generally made evident at some point. I was usually willing to wait. This, though, was ridiculous. What purpose could there be for closing the school? Yep, I was definitely getting attitude.

I looked up at the sky and made a face at whatever powers were up there. "Thanks!" I muttered. "Thanks a lot."

I left the Jeep reluctantly, wondering how I would manage to smile and act like everything was okay. Pausing outside the battered wooden door at the back of the restaurant, I tried on a smile and cleared my mind. The kids had to come first. I would focus on them and not what the future held. They deserved that.

I guess I wasn't fooling Father Sephria that afternoon. He stayed for the entire spelling class, even taking over the signing for Emilio and Carter so I didn't have to sign as I taught—a good thing as Sally was acting up and wouldn't take her turn defining the words from Tuesday. I didn't give her the usual time-out because I felt certain all of them were picking up on the tension filtering through all the teachers in the school. I set them on the task of reading over their next unit while Father Sephria and I retreated to the back of the room.

"So what did she say?" he asked in his heavily accented English. His deep brown eyes searched my face intently.

"Nothing changed," I replied. "She said it was a done deal. We have till the first of April."

"*Dios mío*," he said, crossing himself. "What will we do?"

"Close the school. We have no choice."

"There has to be a church that will allow us to use it," he said with conviction.

"Every weekday? I don't know about that. And what about access for the wheelchairs and Freddy's hospital bed? You know how old the churches are around here."

He shook a finger at me. "No bad allowed!" he scolded.

I had to smile at him. "You're right, Padre, no pessimism allowed. Something good will happen."

"Yes, I will pray. God will see us through."

I glanced back at the class, at the kids with their heads bent over their textbooks. "We'll all pray...while we pack."

His disapproving *tsk* followed me when I returned to my students.

GREY

A quick glance at the green glowing face on my alarm clock told me it was three in the morning. I lay very still, trying to discern what sound had awakened me. There it was again, a low growl. I rose slowly and peered along the hall that led into the living room. In the dim light coming from the condominium streetlights, I saw Oscar Marie crouched low, her ears back, facing the doorway that led into the Bookmark.

I started to call to her, then experienced a sudden, clutching fear. Suppose someone had succeeded in breaking in again? I had reset the alarm system with another new code, but suppose it had been circumvented somehow?

I picked up a flannel shirt from next to the bed and shrugged into it while I unplugged my cell phone so I could carry it with me. I stepped carefully across the bedroom and into the carpeted hallway. I would not call the Port Isabel Police Department again until I knew something definite. I'd felt so foolish yesterday when they'd found no evidence of a break-in. I could tell by their actions that they thought me a loopy, hysterical female, overreacting and not even remembering what I had done or not done.

Yet I knew without a doubt that I had not stacked the books that way. They had been neatly placed in vertical alignment. The policeman who responded first had caused me to briefly doubt myself, but after he and the second officer left, I retraced my steps in my mind and knew what I had done. But no door locks had been breached, and the windows were all still securely locked from the inside.

Approaching the kitchen, I silently slid a butcher knife from the knife block and approached the door into the front room. Oscar Marie meowed her concern to me, but I ignored her and quietly turned the knob with my left hand, taking care that my cell phone didn't knock against it.

The door squealed when it opened, so I reached in right away and flipped on all three toggles for the house lights. Sudden, blinding brightness from the ceiling lights made me squint my eyes into tight slits, but I still searched the room for an intruder.

I saw no one. Oscar Marie raced past me and paused just past the first coffee counter to arch her back and hiss. Her fur had bristled up all over her body. My first thought was that one of Maddy's dogs had somehow found its way back here, and then I thought of a raccoon, or a rat. There simply had to be something there.

I renewed my grip on the knife handle and leaned across the coffee bar to see if there was anything behind it. There wasn't anyone or anything large back there, but my view was limited by my angle. I slowly moved forward, prepared to dart away if I saw anything threatening. Nothing. As I stood there, perplexed, glancing at Oscar Marie, a blanket of coldness washed over me, a coldness like I'd never felt before. It wasn't like weather, like a draft, but rather something that clung to my skin like rubber and instantly chilled me to the core.

I gasped at the sudden onslaught. The knife tumbled from my abruptly numb fingers. Immediately, the coldness disappeared and I took a deep, shuddering breath.

"Mary," I whispered, seeing an image of her in my mind. Clearing my throat, I spoke louder. "Mary, is that you?"

My Swedish mother had always sworn her belief in ghosts, in the restless spirits that walk our realm, but until that moment I had never experienced anything that even smacked of the supernatural. I doubted the experience, but knew there would be no cold breeze naturally. The South Texas nights were balmy.

I let my gaze roam the room. Had Mary left me some sort of sign? What did the stacks of books mean? Was she trying to get them back? Enjoy them from the other side just as she had while alive?

Seeing nothing, I hung my head in frustration. "Mary," I whispered once more, sadness rebounding within me.

After some time, I turned helplessly to return to my apartment. Lifting my gaze again, I noticed a book spread open on the bookshelf behind the coffee bar. I hurried over to see if there was some possible message from Mary.

Goddess Annalise
The gift of you
Clenches
Draws the soul of me into you.
Light dawns in your smile and night

With you makes each day fresh;
lust chases itself

As need for you simmers
And cooks me into
A new stew

Eat of me and
we grow as one

I studied the poem until my brow grew tired from being curved into a bow. It made no sense. I understood the passion of it, but the name Annalise meant absolutely nothing to me.

I closed the book and had a moment of déjà vu. This was the same book that had been moved my first day at the Bookmark. Titled *Abandoned*, it was by an author, a poet, named Eleanor Copeland. I thumbed through the small hardbound volume, trying to jog my memory.

I'd never heard of this author nor recognized any of her work. I was not surprised. The copyright date was 1952, way before my time. Why would Mary choose to talk to me with this volume out of the many thousands here? Why not a poet we both enjoyed, like Emily Dickinson or Elizabeth Browning?

Oscar Marie purred below me and rubbed my bare legs with her silky fur. She seemed to have returned to normal, no longer afraid.

"I don't know, baby girl." I sighed. I looked around the room again, suddenly feeling very alone. Obviously, my Mary had gone somewhere else.

"Back to bed for us." I noted the page the poem was on, closed the book, and replaced it on the shelf. I shepherded Oscar Marie back into the apartment and switched off the Bookmark lights. It was a long time before I fell back asleep.

Mary's haunting seemed like a strange, meandering dream the next morning as I dressed and made my way into Brownsville to run errands. I tried to push the night's strangeness from my mind while I focused on furniture needs and coffeemakers.

Brownsville, the southernmost city in the state of Texas, is only about twenty miles from the Gulf waters. Big and sprawling, it has a definite easygoing, Hispanic influence, even though it offers a large, busy, international port. According to the brochure I cribbed off the counter at one of the furniture stores I visited, the city was actually carved from Matamoros, a city in the Mexican state of Tamaulipas. All I noted while driving around the business district was that even the modernized area had a prominent sense of history about it.

Leaving the city proper, I saw an access road, and following signs, decided to explore the Old Port Road. I traveled along Highway 48 which took me through the port and industrial areas. Both sides of the road were dominated by huge, nondescript warehouses.

My curiosity made me want to stop, but the heavy security, highly evident, put me off. This was no place for the casual passer-by. I saw several restaurants that catered to the large industrial workforce as well as a few small convenience stores. When the long road ended, I found to my delight that I'd made a big circle and was back on Highway 100, the road that led past my home and over to the island.

I turned right. Going past the Bookmark and other businesses at Lighthouse Square, I drove across the two-mile long Queen Isabella Causeway.

The drive across the long, regally sloping bridge had to be one of the most beautiful sights known to man. Choppy bay and ocean water, bearing the characteristic dusky, clay-based blue of South Texas waterways, beckoned on both sides while brightly colored banners on the bridge and the accompanying long fishing piers lent a festive air to the journey. I'd heard how crowded the island became during spring break, but right now, during the month before, traffic was sparse and I was across and onto the island quickly.

Gaining South Padre Island's now familiar main street, I turned left and proceeded down the center of the island. Turning onto the road that fronted the powerful Gulf of Mexico, within minutes I was at a wide beach access behind a small thatched hotel called The Surfer's Stay.

The hotel was only three stories, much smaller than the towering hotels on either side. It had a warm, welcoming air. I was greeted with friendly catcalls from a table full of rowdy partiers at the open-air bar on the water. I smiled and waved to them, and made my way down the sand dunes until I stood next to the battering waves.

I stood a good while, allowing the harsh ocean wind to push against me. I took a deep breath and allowed my mind to dwell on the events of the night before.

I felt cheated and angry. I couldn't even believe that my Mary would do this to me, torture me with her love, so close but so inevitably far away. I had begun to feel hopeful that healing had a chance, even though I knew I was far from healed, but I would never forget the pain of my loss while Mary continued to haunt me.

Emptying my mind, I headed north, my sandals dangling from my fingers. I listened as gulls appeared to shout snap counts to one another before arranging into an offensive line.

The water today was a muted blue, different from the bright blue of the day before. It was amazing how the ocean could change its face and demeanor from day to day, sometimes hour to hour. I stood at the water's edge, my eyes following the slow progress of two shrimpers far out on the horizon. I moved on, closing my eyes and savoring the wind on my face.

I suddenly felt a presence next to me and paused. Alarmed, I opened my eyes to see the scowling countenance of a young Hispanic youth. His dark eyes bored into me. He stood less than a foot away. I could smell his strong, earthy scent, even in the pounding wind.

He made strange gestures with his hands, and then grasped me by the shoulders, trying to push me down to the sand. I gasped in fear which rapidly changed to outrage. I knocked his hands away, but with a grim expression, he grabbed me yet again.

He made odd grunting noises and simply would not let go. I pushed at him again and we grappled. Realizing he was stronger and would soon overpower me, I swept his legs out from under him, a technique I had learned in self-defense courses.

"What the hell are you doing? If you've hurt him, I'll have your butt in jail so fast..."

I turned and saw an athletic blonde shouting and racing angrily toward me. I recoiled and lifted my hands to my face. It was the same woman who had dumped pizza on me at The Fat Mother restaurant. What would she do to me now?

ANGIE

It was a perfect day for a beach outing, even if only for the hour we stole from the end of the school day.

The sky was a pure pale blue with just enough cloud to make it interesting, and the sun was a golden glow on its descent toward evening. I guided the Jeep into a parking space at Billy's beach access and quieted everyone for a quick pep talk about safety and staying together as a group. Tommy had gotten hyper on the trip over, as he always did when riding in the open-air Jeep, and I had to give him a few stern looks to calm him during my warning speech, but I think everyone got the importance of staying safe. Besides, they knew the drill from previous trips. My overprotectiveness was just that—overprotectiveness.

It was only the mobile kids with me today anyway. The wheelchair kids would be riding out with Father Sephria when he came in the van to pick these kids up for their ride home.

I had actually been hoping for some beach time all week. I think we all needed a little R and R right about now.

"Miss Angie?" Maria had fallen in step with me while the others ran ahead to chase the retreating waves.

I rested my hand on one of her slim shoulders. "Um-hmm?"

"The school is closing, isn't it?"

Her voice was so quavery and light that I almost couldn't discern the words. "Let's not go there just yet, Maria."

"I'm..."

I paused and turned her so that she faced me. "What, hon? Tell me what you're thinking."

Her long, dark hair hung in her face to hide the scar that marred her right cheek. My hands itched to pull back the thick hair so I could see both her eyes, but I knew that would make her uncomfortable. I took a chance, though, and laid a hand on the bare skin of her arm. My body jolted uncontrollably when I felt the cold steel of a knife against my throat. I jerked the hand away, but I had also felt her question and knew her fear.

"We'll figure something out, Maria. You won't have to go to regular school. I promise I won't let that happen." I made her see me, see my truth. "Don't be afraid. Trust me on this."

She nodded, and I saw a smile curve her lips. "Better watch out."

I turned just as a shirttail full of sand landed on my sandaled feet. Tommy had talked Sally into holding out the hem of her T-shirt so he could load it with sand. They were huddling back and giggling uncontrollably.

"Tommy, I know you were the mastermind of this one," I said as I lifted each foot and tried to shake the sand off.

"Mastermind," he muttered behind the hands pressed to his mouth, ineffectively holding the hilarity in.

I turned my head around and glared at Sally. "Do you even know what your mother is going to do to me when she sees that shirt?"

Sally looked down as if just now realizing how peppered with sand her shirt was. She looked up and I saw a storm of tears brewing.

"Oh, no, honey. Don't *cry*! Look, we can brush it off..."

Her chubby little hands started scrubbing at the shirt. I leaned to help.

"Oh, no," Tommy called. "Someone's *hurting* him!"

I whirled to see that Emilio was under attack. "Watch them," I told Maria as I rushed to rescue Emilio.

"What the hell are you doing? If you've hurt him, I'll have your butt in jail so fast..."

I took a double take. It was *her*! My future wife. I had been wondering when I would see her again. But she had thrown Emilio to the ground and was standing over him, her chest heaving. What in the world?

I took a minute to study her. Dressed in walking shorts and a sleeveless tank top, delicate leather sandals trailing from one of her hands, she was still gorgeous. She looked tired, with dark smudges under her eyes, and had an absentminded air about her.

I approached slowly and leaned over to pull Emilio up off the sand.

GREY

I stopped in my tracks and studied the delivery girl. She was different today, less severe, her unruly hair in a loosely fastened ponytail. She wore baggy khaki shorts and a crew neck shirt in navy blue. The color enhanced the depth of hue in her blue eyes. I found myself admiring the strong lines of her face.

She approached and helped the boy to his feet, then looped an arm protectively about his shoulders. She eyed me angrily. "Why are you beating up on Emilio?"

My jaw dropped. "What? *He* attacked *me*! For no good reason."

The blonde cocked her hip and folded her arms across her chest. "Oh, I am so sure. He doesn't know you from Adam."

Her sarcastic tone hit a nerve. "And I don't know him. If this is your son, and you're going to let him wander the beach alone, maybe you should teach him how to behave."

The blue eyes widened in surprise, then clouded so I knew my remark had hit home. Emilio, who had been following the conversation by peering intently at each of us in turn, started gesticulating wildly. I backed away. The fair woman watched him intently before she gestured in return. I realized suddenly that they were speaking in sign language. I sighed in dismay. Obviously, the youth had been trying to tell me something.

The woman shook her head and smiled. She gestured once more to Emilio then came toward me.

"Come with me," she said, her gaze meeting mine.

A strange thing happened. As I gazed into her eyes, I felt something push my curiosity about what she was going to say clean away. I had an absurd urge to touch her, and had to clasp both hands together so I wouldn't. I looked away, afraid of the intensity of the feelings welling in me. Ridiculous.

She turned and walked a few feet. "This is what he was warning you about."

I followed her pointing finger and saw a long swath of jellyfish in a vertical arch that traversed my path. I would have stepped on them, especially with my eyes closed.

I glanced back at the boy. He stood, his fingers nervously flipping the hem of his shirt. I felt awful. I lifted my eyes to the woman's and knew she realized I'd meant him no harm. I still felt compelled to explain to her. I didn't. Instead, I moved toward the boy.

"Emilio. Forgive me. I didn't mean to misunderstand." I positioned myself so he could clearly see my lips. He brightened and hung his head as if much younger than his teenaged years. I tapped his chin, bringing his gaze back to mine. "Thank you for saving me from a lot of pain."

"Well, I guess you're not as mean as I originally thought," the blonde said from behind me.

I stiffened. "I can show you mean, if that's what you prefer," I said, turning around slowly, ready for battle.

The woman held up her hands, spread apart as if to show me her good intentions. She smiled. Though miffed at her, I couldn't prevent my own small grin in return.

"What, no pizza today?" I asked.

She blushed a fierce red and shook her head. "I am so, so sorry about that. I can be such a klutz sometimes."

"No harm done," I said as several young people approached us. "It was a nice welcome to the area."

"What happened?" asked a young boy. His speech was slurred by an overlarge tongue, but I understood him easily. He peered quizzically at me through thick glasses.

"Everything's okay, Tommy," the blonde told him. "Emilio was trying to warn this nice lady about the jellyfish. What do we know about jellyfish, especially the blue ones?"

"Don't touch," said a young girl with a heavy mane of flaxen hair. She wore thick glasses as well. Her face was round and seemed to encircle a continuous smile.

"That's right, Sally," the woman said, nodding sagely.

I watched them, and suddenly realized that the woman had to be a teacher of special needs kids. I wondered why they were walking the beach instead of working in the classroom. Some type of field trip?

"Look, let's try this again," the woman said, extending her hand. "Let's forget about the pizza and about today. Hello. Welcome to South Padre. I'm Angie June."

I was held static by the tractor beam of her smile. It did exist—that legend of the all-American Beauty. With wisps of pale blond hair framing her face, sparkling blue eyes, and a huge smile filled with white teeth, Angie certainly fit the stereotype. On autopilot, I extended my hand even though my brain was strangely disconnected. I was totally distracted by her wholesome good looks.

"My name is Grey," I stuttered. "Grey Graham."

"That's an interesting name," she said, cocking her head to one side.

I blinked, trying to regroup my senses so I could converse intelligently. "It's an old family name on my mother's side. I guess it could have been worse."

She watched me strangely. I suddenly worried that I'd said something totally different than what I'd meant to say. Just as I opened my mouth to try to salvage the situation, a shout carried to us. We turned together. I saw a short, dark-skinned Hispanic man with a thick graying mustache and a balding head rushing toward us across the sand.

"Oh, no," Angie said, cupping a hand above her eyes to shield out the sun. "That's Father Sephria. I forgot all about him." She turned back to me. "We were supposed to be on our way to meet him when Emilio waylaid you."

I nodded stupidly, only pretending to know what was going on. Angie moved to meet him, followed by the small swarm of young people. One young woman, her dark hair shielding most of her face, lingered behind, peering intently at me through her veil of hair. I smiled at her and she tucked her head shyly and moved after them, her loose shorts flapping in the wind.

I faced a real dilemma. Should I move on, or wait? Angie hadn't said goodbye, but certainly she had more important things to do than talk with me. I cast one more glance her way, lingering on her sturdy, upright form. She was laughing with the priest as the youths milled about them. She was the picture of the perfect woman.

I dropped my gaze and moved on, carefully skirting the surf rolled jellyfish. I tried to plan, to map out my future, but thoughts of Angie's bright blue eyes kept interfering. I smiled to myself. I was attracted to her. It felt nice, but frightening. I wasn't ready. Guilt nagged at me. What right did I have to be attracted to such a vibrant, alive creature when my Mary was...I stopped and hot tears formed. I turned toward the ocean and allowed the wind to snatch them away.

"Do you like beer?"

I whirled around. Angie stood next to me, her approach masked by the roar of the breakers. She too faced the water, studying it with unusual intensity.

"Where are the kids?" I asked, my voice hoarse.

"I turned them over to the padre. He's taking the van back to the center."

"The center?"

"Walk with me and I'll tell you all about it. Do you like shrimp?"

I laughed at her popcorn approach to conversation. "Yes, I like shrimp *and* beer. Why do you ask?"

"Because," she began as she gently steered me along the beach. "I'm hungry and my bud Couscous has some of the best beer battered shrimp you'll ever eat. And his beer is just the way you want it here on the island—frigid." She laughed.

The sound comforted me like a warm bubble bath. I wanted to hesitate, wanted to run from this new involvement when I simply wanted to be alone in my grief, but I couldn't. Angie was enchanting and irresistible, like some force of nature. Saying no to her would be like trying to prevent the burgeoning of spring.

ANGIE

I felt Grey's uncertainty. My memory recalled the vivid image of her sadness. Shaking her hand and opening myself allowed me to know how much she loved being here on South Padre. I also saw confusion and guilt, emotions that perplexed me. She was certainly a complicated woman.

I watched her out of the corner of my eye as I helped Father Sephria load the kids into the van. Delicia handed me a picture she had drawn of a knight on a horse, part of our Middle Ages unit. It was a very good picture.

I snagged a pen from the padre's shirt pocket when he passed by and turned the paper over. I pressed it against the side of the van so I could write on it: *Delicia was a remarkable student today, Mrs. Gonzales.* I drew a few sloppy stars around my note and handed it back to the twelve-year-old. She read it and smiled at me. I winked at her and slid the van door closed.

"Y'all have a safe trip, Father," I said after I walked around to the passenger window and handed him the pen. "I'll be in tomorrow afternoon for English."

"See you then," he said as he put the van into gear. I waved to each of the children as they passed by me, laughing at the comical face Tommy offered.

I turned my attention back to the beach and saw that Grey was walking away. The feeling of her retreating from me was brutal, like a punch dead center into my solar plexus. I took a moment to ponder my extreme sureness that we would be together. This was a first for me, although I'd been in several relationships before. Her aura, even though it was—as are all auras—wispy and undefined, still drew me to her.

I envisioned a five pointed star in my mind, representing the five elements of life, and touched on each point. Earth was the physical plane and certainly our proximity had finally come together as it should. Air, a mystery as yet undefined. I remembered her wit in the restaurant. She seemed intelligent, but only spending time with her would answer that aspect fully. Fire. Oh, yes, her body appealed to me and had already awakened mine. Her spirit was fiery as well, evidenced by her earlier encounter with Emilio. Would this translate into the bedroom? Another mystery. Water. The emotion was there. Her sadness was the first thing I had gleaned from her and I knew her well of emotion ran very deeply. Akasha. The fire spirit of humanity. Would our value systems mesh properly?

I studied her as she turned her face to the water. If they did, then yes, I could cherish this woman forever. But the first steps needed to be taken. I ambled toward her through the sand.

GREY

Within moments, we approached two large hotels separated by a wide alley. I followed Angie into this alley. We fetched up on a low thatched building dwarfed by the towering hotels on the right and left. A sign hanging crookedly across the front of the thatching proclaimed it as Spunky's Puddle.

A half-dozen worn plastic tables and chairs dotted a large square of wooden decking in front of the business, and a similar handful of chairs butted up against a two-tiered bar toward the back. Several of the bar chairs were occupied, but the other tables rested in solitude. Angie took my hand and helped me navigate the tricky sand-obscured steps and step up onto the decking.

The bartender, a large bearded bear of a man, obviously knew Angie and greeted her with genuine enthusiasm.

"Donny, this is my new bud, Grey. Grey, this is Donny, the law and order at the Puddle," Angie explained as she made the introduction.

"An easier job these days," said Donny, taking my hand and clasping it warmly. "Winter Texan season is over for a few months. Now I just need to survive spring break."

He studied me so I felt compelled to provide some information of my own. "I moved here last week from Dallas. This is such a beautiful area, I can't believe I didn't visit it more often."

"Dallas! I *knew* it," Angie said, slapping a palm on the bar.

"Life sure ties us up, doesn't it?" Donny responded to me, eyeing Angie with a lifted brow. "That's why one day I says to myself, 'Don, my friend, it's about time.' So here I am, lots poorer, but lots happier."

I nodded. Donny was living my old dream, the one I'd harbored just about every working day. Now the dream was mine to hold, but at the ultimate cost of losing Mary.

"Is he here?" Angie asked quietly.

"Yeah, got in about noon." Donny carefully scrubbed his fingers with the bar towel.

"Cool." She tentatively reached for my hand. I clasped hers without thought, thrilling at the warmth and strength of her touch.

She paused and studied me intently for a matter of seconds before pulling me along one side of the bar and into an odd little vestibule set into one side of the building. I saw now that the structure was long and low with the same basic footprint as some of the larger surrounding hotels. We passed along a walkway decorated with large wind chimes crafted from oddly shaped, plate-sized pieces of metal attached to thick cord. The sound of the clashing metal surrounded us before being snatched away by the heavy sea wind that buffeted the space where we walked.

Angie paused before an ornate door made of rusted metal, obviously a salvaged piece. She opened the door, setting into motion another group of metal and glass wind chimes that hung just inside the door. She stepped through and drew me into a dim cavern, all the while murmuring cautions about watching my step.

I thought it was a museum at first. Indeed, it could have been if not for the uneven wooden planked floor and the rustic cinderblock and stucco walls. The pieces tastefully arranged around the large room were exquisite. My eyes lingered curiously. I pulled back, trying to slow Angie's headlong rush so I could enjoy the work. She seemed to sense my purpose for she released my hand and joined me in studying a large, double life-sized statue of a mother and child sculpted from a beautiful pink and white marbled stone. The stylized mother, curved protectively around her toddler, had been polished to a satiny finish.

"Do you even realize how much it costs to have something like this shipped in from Europe?" Angie whispered.

I turned to her and saw glee sparkling in her blue eyes. I shook my head. "I have no idea," I whispered. "But I bet it's not cheap."

She nodded dramatically. We moved on to an abstract sculpture that appeared to be a swimmer on the crest of a wave. This one was brass with a suggestion of cobalt blue rubbed into the creases of the figure. We walked on, past a social network of women, men, and children, some athletes, others in pensive mode. As we progressed, I noticed that one of the back corners of the room was filled with a huge, broad piece arranged in a massive easy chair. The drone of a television penetrated. When he moved, I suddenly realized that the enormous man was real.

I'd seen large people before, but this man was colossal. I tried not to stare.

He immediately winked at me and extended his left hand. "It's all right, look all you want, lil' bit. Everyone does."

Caught off guard, I laughed nervously as I took the extended hand and shook it awkwardly.

Angie leaned over to kiss the big man on his pouting, Alfred Hitchcock lips. "Couscous, this is my new friend, Grey. Isn't she pretty?"

The two put their heads together and studied me appreciatively.

"That she is, Angie. How the hell you find all the pretty ones, I'll never know." Couscous absently ran sausage-like fingers across his short red hair as I blushed.

"Oh, yeah, like you have a problem with that," she retorted.

Couscous smiled widely, showing a perfect set of white false teeth. "I do all right," he said smugly.

Angie indicated the many invoices spread across the desk to Couscous's right. "Working on the books?"

"Curse of my life," Couscous responded sharply.

With amazing ease, he gained his feet, straightened his billowing shorts and cotton shirt, then swept his large form across the back of the room. Angie wrapped an arm companionably around my shoulders and smiled at me with unconstrained joy. Bewildered, I allowed myself to be moved along behind the big man.

"I don't know why you don't hire someone to do it," Angie muttered to his retreating back.

"Oh, yeah. I am so gonna trust someone else with my money," he replied sarcastically.

Couscous moved sideways through a wide doorway. We followed him into the largest, most spacious kitchen I'd ever seen. And the most elaborately equipped. Obviously, this really was a restaurant and he worked here.

An elderly, wizened woman of Hispanic descent turned from the sink and smiled at us, her dark eyes twinkling. She had an untidy mop of salt-and-pepper hair piled on her head, and she wore a white apron tied tightly around her body.

"C'lina, mas papas, por favor," Couscous barked, but not unkindly.

The woman nodded and returned Angie's wave. She moved

busily and soon the delicious smell of frying potatoes filled the air.

"That's Carolina," Angie said. "She's amazing."

"Large or small ones today?" Couscous asked as he donned an apron the size of a small bedsheet.

Angie studied me briefly before ordering for both of us. "Small, I think, and can you make some of those little hush puppy thingies I like? They are so good."

An older teenager entered the kitchen and spoke to Carolina in rapid Spanish. She nodded and leapt into even more frenzied activity. The young man saw us and moved to a large family-sized table along the back wall of the kitchen. I noted his handsomeness, his jet-black hair, and smooth olive skin.

"*Aquí, chicas.*" He moved chairs around making an inviting niche for the two of us. Angie indicated that I should be seated. The teen darted over to a coffin-sized, chest-type galvanized cooler and returned with two bottled beers. The opener lay ready on the table. He swooped it up, and soon I enjoyed beer cold enough to contain ice crystals. It was the most delicious thing I think I'd ever tasted.

"Thank you, Stevie," Angie said, slapping hands with him.

Stevie smiled. I liked the way his even white teeth flashed in the bright kitchen. "*De nada. Disfrute su comida.*" He hurried off.

Couscous stood at the eight-burner stove, magically juggling several large pots and skillets. Stevie paused to firmly slap the man's wide rump as he left the kitchen. Couscous bellowed good-naturedly after him.

"Stevie?" I studied Angie's face as she took a long swig of the frosty beer.

She laughed and shrugged. "One of Couscous's dozen."

"Dozen? What do you mean?"

Angie laughed. "Kids. He has like, four wives and a dozen kids at last count."

"Are you serious?" I examined him, wondering at the attraction.

"Yep. Go figure. They adore him, wives and kids both."

"Isn't that, like...illegal?"

She grinned as she extended her hand palm down and wiggled it. "Legal shmegal."

I nodded my understanding as a short, but very curvy Hispanic woman entered the kitchen and hailed Couscous, pausing to lay a kiss on him. She wore large hoop earrings and her glossy black hair was pulled back into a neat ponytail. She wore skintight jeans and pale green heels, and her green knit shirt clung tightly to her body.

"Sanchez!" Angie called, rising and beckoning. "Come have a beer with us."

The woman named Sanchez smiled and hurried over. She pulled up a chair next to Angie and her snapping black eyes studied me curiously.

"*¡Hola, amiga, que son de una belleza hoy, si!*" she said dramatically.

Angie blushed and made the introductions. "Sanchez, this is my friend, Grey Graham. She just moved here from Dallas. Grey, this is Anna Sanchez, one of my oldest and dearest friends."

We shook hands. Sanchez started telling me about how much she loved Dallas and how she, her sisters, and mother went to Dallas three times a year to shop for clothing because they had the best selection. Angie rose and fetched a beer for Sanchez as Sanchez grilled me on where I had lived and what I had done while living near Dallas.

"What are you doing so dressed up?" Angie asked when there was a small lull in our intense conversation. "And on your day off."

"I went and saw *mi corazon*," she said with a coy smile. "He is so *guapo*, makes my teeth hurt."

"Anna has taken up with a much older businessman," Angie explained. "Who just so happens to have a yacht down at Spencer's Marina and they spend a lot of time there."

"Ah," I said, nodding in understanding.

Sanchez looked at me again and leaned toward Angie. "*Una muchacha muy bonita. ¿Te amaba todavía?*"

"That's none of your damned business," Angie replied, nudging Sanchez away.

We quieted when a young couple entered the room. The man, in his twenties, bore familiar red hair and possessed a stocky body much like his father's. The tall woman with him was full-figured as well and carried an infant.

"Hey, Papa!" the man called out as he clasped hands and bumped bellies with his father. They exchanged pleasantries. The young man snatched an apron off the wall. After a quick stop to fetch a bowl from the huge two-door industrial refrigerator, he moved to help Carolina at the deep fryer. The woman and child spied us and moved close as Angie rose and rushed to meet them. She took the baby from the woman's arms and they embraced.

"Grey, this is Yvette, Brian's wife." She nuzzled the baby, making her giggle. "And mother to this little imp, Georgie girl."

I nodded to Yvette, noting how pretty she was with thick, dark hair pulled back into a ponytail, and large brown eyes. "Hello, Yvette."

"Hey, Anna, Hey, Grey. Most just call me Vetty," she told me.

She pulled a chair from a line of them resting against a nearby wall and took a seat next to me at the table. Angie pulled over a high chair, but sat and stood the baby on her thighs, still cooing and making funny faces at the child. Sanchez leaned to coo to the baby in Spanish.

"Ah, New York?" I asked Vetty. Her accent was distinctive.

She laughed. "Brooklyn. You know the area?"

"Not really. Just went to school with a gal from up that way." I watched Angie interact with the baby. She was a natural with kids, I could tell.

"It's real different from here," she offered.

"I think South Texas is like no place else anyway," I added. "How did you end up here?"

"Dad's an oil rigger, and he didn't like the schools in Corpus, so he moved me, my mom, and my brother down here so we could go to better schools."

"And that's how she met Brian," Sanchez explained, all the while making ridiculous expressions to make the baby laugh. Vetty was a talker. I soon knew all about her life chasing oil through the state of Texas with her family when she was younger. When the food came, I stared at the lovely offerings as if held spellbound by a snake charmer—huge baskets of brown, steaming hush puppies, mounds of golden french fries, and a heaping platter of fried shrimp, artfully arranged with lemon wedges and small, dark green bowls of cocktail sauce.

Couscous was like an alchemist in the kitchen. I'm not sure what he did to the food, but I ate like a fiend until I thought my stomach would burst. I hadn't enjoyed eating much since Mary died, but this food was irresistibly delicious. All of us had a healthy appetite. Soon, the table looked like a war zone, yet Carolina brought over even more food—a stainless pot full of boiled shrimp, heavily coated with a spicy powder. Though ready to burst, I had to try just one. I groaned at the beauty of it.

Angie's and Sanchez's laughter made me blush.

"Oh, yeah," Angie intoned. "Welcome to the island. Spunky's has *the* best food."

"I agree," said Vetty, leaning back and patting her tummy. She looked over at Georgie, who was gumming a teething biscuit into a smeared mess. It was even in her hair. "Your turn's coming, little bit," she said. Georgie offered a biscuit-adorned grin in return and pounded the treat on the high chair tray, apparently in hearty agreement.

I noted that food was regularly going out of the kitchen as the three of us ate, so I was not too surprised to see that the outdoor tables were mostly filled with customers when Angie and I left the back kitchen part of the restaurant.

"Sanchez seems nice. And I like Vetty, too," I said as we made our way onto the beach.

After Sanchez departed, we had left Vetty cleaning up the table while Georgie babbled from her perch in the high chair. I felt guilty for not helping, but she shooed us out and informed us that she was supposed to be working anyway because she was being paid.

"Yeah, Anna and I go way back, and if you ask me, all Couscous's clan are good people. Without a doubt."

"I agree. They wouldn't even let us pay anything for all that food."

"Yeah," she sighed. "He's pretty aggravating about that."

We walked on the cool, hard-packed sand just beyond the water's edge. The insistent wind seemed bent on forcing our bodies into one another.

"How did you meet him? Couscous," I clarified.

She laughed and leaned into me so I could hear her over the wind and waves. "I met him when he was about three hundred pounds lighter. He came into town from Las Vegas and Mama hired him as a chef at the restaurant."

"Figures," I responded. "Did he work there long?"

"A couple years. Unbeknownst to us, he was a huge lotto player, and lo and behold, one day he won the Texas State Lottery."

I stared at her. "No way!"

She shook her head as if bewildered. "Yes, way. A couple million."

"And he opened a restaurant?"

She shrugged. "What can I say? He loves to cook."

We laughed together. I realized it had been a long, long time since I had felt this relaxed and so completely at ease.

"May I hug you goodbye?" Angie asked me abruptly when we reached my car.

I pondered the question. Not the idea of the hug, but rather that she felt she had to ask. I smiled and held out my arms. "Of course."

She drew me into her embrace. My body fell limp, reacting immediately to the powerful strength I felt in her. Her body was strong. Though probably a ridiculous notion, I felt her spirit was strong too. She held me gently, a hand firmly cradling my shoulder. Comfort washed across me...and attraction. I held her tightly, my head tucked into the curve of her neck, and imagined being loved again.

We held each other longer than might be considered seemly, and I know my cheeks were pink when I finally stepped back. She didn't seem to notice. She waited while I unlocked the door, got inside my car, and started the engine.

"Thank you, for everything," I said when I rolled down the window. "You still owe me a story, though, about the...the center?"

"Oh, yeah, I forgot. Come by the restaurant sometime when you can," she called. She moved to one side and swung herself into a bright yellow Jeep. "I'm there most mornings and evenings."

I waved to show I'd heard.

I drove home pensively, thinking about Angie the whole way. I loved the way her nose crinkled when she laughed, and how her lips and eyebrows were a pale flaxen color bleached even lighter by the sun's energy. I also loved to study the patterns made by the light freckles that peppered her cheeks. The gamine contours of her face were enchanting. I realized with some amazement that I couldn't wait to see her again.

ANGIE

I'd felt her. Really felt her, and she was an amazing person. I wasn't sure what a "Suzy deadline" was, but everything else I'd picked up from my hug with Grey Graham had proven what I had surmised about her from that very first day.

I saw that she had recently lost "Mary," someone she'd been very close to. Was it a partner? I wasn't sure, but I knew that I needed to get to know her on this earthly plane. I set that as a new, short-term life goal on the drive home.

My small cottage on the causeway side of North Shore may

have been small, but I had been really comfortable there since moving from Cathy's apartment. I'd never been much on having a lot of stuff. It seemed like I was happy with all the stuff that nature provided me outside, so some would have considered my living style to be extremely minimalistic.

Mama, the packrat of the family, said it was just sad. She attributed it to me avoiding the energies I picked up from objects. I suppose some of that was true. All I was sure of is that I wasn't willing to expend energy on things that weren't important to me.

After letting in Buddy, the neighborhood's stray cat, I put some food in his bowl and relaxed on the sofa, staring out at the sun-bleached scrub grass beyond my sliding glass door. The ocean was ten feet from the door, but the soothing water just wouldn't distract me today.

I listened to Buddy crunching his dry food and absently mewing enjoyment to himself, and let my thoughts roam. This could be a risky endeavor as, when fully relaxed, often too much information creeps in. I'd learned as a child to dampen down my intuitive abilities and I carried that self-made buffer around daily. Only at home alone would I let my guard down, and even then I picked up some pretty weird messages from time to time.

I would always remember when Cerise Hernandez came to me. She'd been dead six months and had been bothered the entire time by her mother's extreme grief. She wanted me to let everyone know where her body could be found so that her mother would accept her death and get on with her own life. That had been a bit freaky. I'd done as she asked, leading the police to her body, accidentally entombed in a refrigerator when hiding from her brother, but I wanted those on the other side to know I wasn't in the business of carrying messages for them. I needed to keep both feet firmly on the side of the living, so I ignored a lot when I was open.

Leaning forward, I lit the thick candle resting in the center of my coffee table. It was a good focal point, helping sharpen my thoughts so they would go where I wanted them to go and not where they were pulled. Today, I wanted to think about the SPICEY and about Grey.

I sensed huge changes coming in my life. Unfortunately, I was better with static energies from the past rather than visions of the future, so those upcoming changes would remain a mystery until they transpired.

I stared at the candle and focused on what Frankee had said, that maybe it was time to let the school close. Was that a message I should take to heart?

The kids I taught were all special needs kids, students who could be reasonably mainstreamed into the regular public school system. But would they be happy there? Their parents and I agreed on this one fact: probably not. There were a lot of fine teachers in Port Isabel schools. The problem is they were all overworked and underpaid. When it took me six tries to gain Tommy's attention so he could soak up one important fact, it was evident that other teachers were just being set up to fail these kids. No, we had to keep the school open. The problem was *how*?

I thought about a fundraiser or a grant. Would that give us enough time to get the word out and get the funds in? I doubted it. So what to do? My meager salary was paid by a grant and the parents paid a stiff activities fee already. As I had so many times before, I would wait. Wait for the issue to resolve the way it would while shifting energies as far in what I considered the direction of right and correct as I could.

Buddy approached the sofa. I leaned forward to give him a few quick scratches before he had to head back outside to patrol his territory. He never stayed long. I rose and let him out through the glass doors.

I followed him outside and strolled down to the water's edge. My neighbor, Jimmy Carson, was about a quarter mile out in water that came almost to the top of his waders. He saw me and waved.

"Fishing for a late supper?" I called to him.

"You know it," he called back cheerfully and recast his line. "Red snapper are running."

I looked down and watched a sea hare undulate by in its indigo-purple beauty. Ducks over by the breakwater disagreed violently and let everyone know about it with their loud calls. I thought of Grey and wondered if she would come to love me. We'd had such a good afternoon together, and I had sensed her reacting positively to me. Hope swelled in my heart. I wish we'd been alone, so I could have talked with her more intimately. I couldn't see the future, but I did see feelings. And they were there. Growing slowly, but there. I hugged myself and lifted my eyes to the horizon, trying to feel Grey again.

GREY

I'm not 100 percent sure why you came to Marks & Crocker, Suzy.
I was denied a raise at my other job, sir.
Ah, yes, receptionist for that financial firm downtown.
Yes, sir, that's the one.
But you're a very good worker, Suzy, I can't understand that.
My manager decided I was slacking. He said every time he saw me,
I was either chatting with someone in the lobby or talking on the phone.

I studied my scribbled notes for the comic strip and wondered if the joke was too subtle. I leaned back and yawned, hoping that I would get a good night's sleep tonight. I rubbed Oscar Marie's ears. She was on her usual perch on the flat, narrow surface at the back top of my drafting table. She purred with delight.

"Let's try and sleep through the night tonight, old girl," I told her. I glanced at the closed door to the Bookmark, refusing to dwell on the night before.

I looked back at the strip and lifted my two main markers.

I had always enjoyed drawing Suzy. In fact, the character with her dark page boy and overlarge glasses had been one of the first characters I had doodled while still a young child. The name had been the same then too, but over the years, she had worked many different careers as a nurse, a stewardess, and at times a firefighter and a doctor. In fact, I wasn't sure there wasn't any career she hadn't attempted at least once.

For the past ten years, though, she had been cemented in as a receptionist for the Marks & Crocker legal firm. Now I suppose she would be there forever. Syndication had a way of stagnating a strip. Now it was up to me to bring her to life each week within those confines. Not always an easy task.

Luckily, her boss was a chauvinist idiot and Suzy herself, well, I liked to say she was a little clueless most of the time.

I started with the final frame. Using a thin black marker, I sketched Suzy sitting at her desk, wearing a headset unplugged from the phone and slung by its skinny black cord over one shoulder. I usually tried to follow Dallas weather patterns and today was a cold day there, so I sketched in a button-down cardigan. Her legs were crossed, and one kitten-heeled pump dangled from the toes of the upper foot, the sight just visible in the kneehole of her desk.

Alexander Marks sat in a rolling office chair on the opposite side of her desk, his legs extended and his feet propped on her desk. She had just delivered her punch line so he was looking at her with a raised disbelieving eyebrow, his characteristic unlit cigar hanging from the corner of his droopy lips. I opened his mouth a little so that the cigar drooped comically. There, that helped. I reached for the correction fluid and all hell broke loose.

Oscar Marie hissed and spit, and the paper panel was pulled from beneath my hands and tossed on the floor. I felt a frigid wind, just like the night before, sweep across me and race away.

I dropped the bottle of correction fluid onto the floor as I backed away from the drafting table. Oscar Marie was standing up on her perch now, her back arched and fur standing up all over her body. I pressed my back against the dining room wall.

"Mary? Honey?" I searched the room. It had to be her. There was no wind coming in from outside and the air-conditioning hadn't kicked on since nightfall.

"Mary? Won't you talk to me, sweetheart? Are...are you angry at me for moving? I kept your books though, all but the ones Brynna took. They're all here."

I waited, willing her to communicate so I could be comforted by her presence instead of afraid. I heard the wind outside, buffeting the exterior of my apartment, but she didn't speak to me.

A low growl sounded from Oscar Marie. The door to the Bookmark clicked open. The slow groan of the door opening set every hair on my body rising. I knew I had shut the door securely before coming back to work, when I had swept the huge expanse of floor one last time, preparing for tomorrow's furniture delivery, and then checked the alarm before switching off all the lights. I had closed that door. Yet it gaped open invitingly, as if waiting for me to come and learn the secrets of the universe. I couldn't move. Terror held my body captive.

Oscar Marie followed her usual descent path from drafting table to dining table to chair to floor. She approached the doorway cautiously, and then moved across the threshold.

"Ossie! Wait!" I cried, my body released from its paralysis.

I stepped to the door and reached for the lights. Before I could flip the switch, however, I was caught and held by the strange tableau before me. In the dimness, backlit by the streetlights of Lighthouse Square, I saw that the books I had left so neatly aligned on the shelves were now stacked in the center of the room in a high vertical column.

I noted movement and saw, to my horror, that the huge heavy stack, some eight feet tall, was suspended off the ground by a good twelve inches. The stack was bobbing in midair.

As I watched, the horizontal volumes began to break away from one another and spin in a strange tornado of books. It spun faster as I watched. Suddenly, one of the books broke away and made a beeline for me. I couldn't move. Thankfully, it passed inches from my head and slammed into the doorframe.

A loud phantom scream fractured the night and woke me from my stupor.

I grabbed Oscar Marie roughly by her collar and scurried into the relative safety of the apartment as more books broke loose from the vortex. I slammed the door shut and felt the vibration of the heavy wood panel as several volumes slammed against it.

I twisted the deadbolt and backed away from the door, holding my breath while I waited for what other new horror would befall me.

ANGIE

Mama and I were both having a hard time waking up this morning. Thank goodness Gail was lively enough for both of us because she was doing most of the setups while Mama and I leaned on the bar, slurping extra coffee.

"So why are you so tired?" I asked her.

She blushed suddenly, causing me to chuckle into my coffee cup.

"That's none of your business, young 'un."

"Hey, that's just fine with me, Mama. You'd best get it while you can." I waved a dismissive hand at her. "So how does Nando look this morning?"

She grinned at me and moved to the back of the bar for more coffee. "Who said anything about Fernando?"

I perked right up. "Mama...something you want to tell me?"

She added extra cream to her cup. "I already told you it was none of your business."

I slid off my stool and moved toward her.

"Oh no, you don't! Don't you dare touch me!" She laughed, the movement causing her white apron to flutter against her abundant chest.

I paused in my advance. Curiosity was chewing a hole in me, but she was my mother and I had to respect that.

"Shoot, Mama, come on!" I begged, stretching an arm toward her.

She laughed at my dilemma, but shook her head firmly.

I backed away and resumed my seat.

"So what's been happening in Angie's world?" she asked when she took her seat next to me.

I looked at her, trying to show my aggravation. "Oh, yeah, like I'm gonna tell you anything now."

She stared me down, her familiar warm brown eyes filled with merriment and demand.

"I met Grey again," I said finally.

"Grey?" She squinted, trying to remember.

"The woman I dumped the pizza on."

"Oh. Which one?"

It took me thirty seconds before I realized she was pulling my leg. "Aw, Mama. Why you gotta be mean? You know I've never dumped a pizza on anyone else."

Her smile was infectious. "I don't know about that. Seems to me when you were just starting out, you let fly a couple."

I ignored her comment, realizing it was true. "So anyway, I ran into her on the beach yesterday. She's awesome. I took her over to Couscous's place, and we had a blast."

Mama smiled a satisfied little smile and leaned forward, showing her interest. "So what's she like?"

I shook my head and focused on the ceiling. "Better than I expected. We didn't get a chance to talk much because Sanchez and Vetty were there, but I got a big old hug when we said good-bye."

Mama sat back and closed her eyes. "I am so happy for you, baby girl. It's about time you found the right one." She rose. I knew our morning laziness was over. "I don't know how you know all these things, but you know I trust you with it," she went on.

She pulled me into a sideways hug. I pressed my cheek to hers and opened myself. I saw the two of them lifting beers at the Puddle. They are the only ones in the place because it is so late. Mama and...*Donny*.

I pulled back and grinned at her. "Ooh, he's hot, Mama. Good for you!"

"Darn you, Angela Rose. I don't know what I'm gonna do with you."

"You know you can't have secrets from me, Mama. Too connected." I paused. "So do you know where she lives? Grey Graham?"

"Now, how would I...?" She paused. I saw memory stir behind her big brown eyes. "Wait a minute...Grey Graham. That's the name of the woman who bought Ruetta's place. Just on the corner here."

As if highlighting her words, a huge truck from Canton Furniture in Brownsville blocked out the morning sunlight when it passed into the square. We quieted and watched the truck in unison as it lumbered by. I looked at Mama and she looked at me.

"Go! Go see," she said, sighing. "But try to get back here soon. Hasty's not coming in until ten."

Unable to hide my delight, I let loose a little squeal and kissed her cheek. "You got it!"

I walked down the Square and there she was, watching nervously while the men tried to position the truck on Maxan so it wouldn't block the entire street. It was a good thing they'd come early. Most of the slanted parking slots were empty and they had more room to maneuver.

Grey saw me. Her face lit with a light that flared her aura into a corona of gold around her head. She waved and I waved back as I made my way over to her.

"I just found out that you bought this place," I told her. "I had no idea."

"Yeah, I did. I live here too, in the back," she said.

"Oh, yeah, Elizondo's home away from home," I said. "You must live alone then, because that place is small."

Her smile faltered a bit. I could have kicked myself for bringing up what had to be a sore issue. I changed the subject quickly. I peered through the window and saw shelved books as far as I could see. "Ah, a bookstore! Cool!"

The smile returned. "Well, sort of. Actually it's a reading room and coffeehouse."

She paused as two men bearing a large easy chair paused behind her.

"Um, you need to go," I said, trying to keep sadness out of my voice. "I guess they need you to tell them where to put everything."

She glanced around. "Yeah," she agreed apologetically.

"I gotta go do breakfast too."

"Come back by later, maybe, when everything is set up."

Her invitation thrilled me, but I remembered suddenly that I had to work. SPICEY first, and then at Mama's.

"It'll be later though, maybe not today. But I will. I'm...I'm really glad you'll be here in Lighthouse Square." I grimaced inwardly. How lame did that sound?

"Thank you," she said, cocking her head to the side. She was adorable. "I'll look forward to seeing you around."

I lowered my head, feeling shy. I muttered something then waved stupidly. I turned and headed back to The Fat Mother. I glanced back once, but Grey had already gone inside.

GREY

I couldn't help myself. I just had to walk through the Bookmark one more time.

I started at the securely bolted front door and strode slowly through my design. It was exactly as I had envisioned. Each of four conversation centers consisted of five chairs curved against the outer wall, with a coffee table set into the curve of the half moon of chairs. Two areas had two small end tables evenly spaced amid the chairs. These held beautiful art-deco lamps. Two others, though laid out the same fashion, had chandelier floor lamps that emitted a soft light at the back and sides of the grouping. The final two, closest to the coffee counters at the back of the store, had large breakfast nook-sized tables slightly higher than the others. These areas offered curved, cushiony bench seating with more modern-looking floor lamps.

The chunky, circular wooden carousels between each conversation area imparted a sense of privacy and gave the huge room some much needed definition. New Oriental rugs, laid end to end, bisected the room and gave it a desirable warmth. Also, it was much quieter. My footsteps no longer echoed when I walked through the room. The only things missing were the chalkboards, the coffeemakers and setups, and the wooden blinds for the four small recessed windows. Then it would be perfect.

I stepped through the open door of the storeroom, which had been transformed. Heavily lined burgundy drapes almost hid the rank of windows on the side and the larger windows to the front. I had hung sheers under the front set so that some light filtered in.

The seating in this room was much the same, some easy chairs with the exception of two plush chaise lounges, both in matching burgundy, and library tables and chairs in the front. Each chaise had a cloth shaded floor lamp, as did each of the random chairs in this room. The chairs in each corner had an end table holding a squat, fat, ceramic lamp with a large shade. The center rug bore a floral pattern in blue and burgundy that totally pulled the room together.

I stepped back into the main hall. I was no interior designer, but I thought I'd done pretty doggone well. I was very happy with the result.

I opened the door to my apartment. After switching off the main light switches, I quaked inside as I looked at the bookshelves, wondering if tonight would be as disturbing as last night. It had taken me most of the morning to re-shelve all the books piled against my door and in the center of the room. The spine and glue of one book had been broken in the attack. Anger had filled me when I saw it. How could Mary do something like that to her own precious books? And try to hurt me? It just didn't make sense. My anger at Mary, and her ridiculous haunting, had carried me through the day, providing the escape hatch I needed to be able to work on the Bookmark when the movers had arrived.

I pushed the door shut and engaged both locks, double-checking that the door was firmly closed and locked.

Sighing, I turned to my drafting table. Only four more days before this strip had to be sent in. I would scan and e-mail it first, and then overnight the original to the distributor so it could be reproduced properly.

I stared out at the bay a few minutes before turning on the long, skinny light over the table. The light obscured the details beyond the closed window, but I could still see the gentle swelling of the waves. Oscar Marie came and took her usual spot, perching above me when I patted the table.

The strip waited patiently for me. Taking up my smaller marker, I seesawed it between my fingers while I pondered my next move.

I had repaired Mister Marks's mouth earlier that morning before the moving men had arrived, and I had written in Suzy's punch line to the right side above her head. Some cartoonists used balloons, but I preferred self-delineated all caps text with a simple line to the person talking if more than one in a panel. When just one person was talking, I usually didn't bother with a line. The position of the talking character's mouth lent clarity.

I moved backward to the next empty panel. I sketched the two in the exact same positions, except Suzy leaned forward, examining a sheet of paper in her hand. Her boss was talking this time. I gave his mouth an intriguing V shape around the ever-present cigar. His eyes were closed while he pontificated, saying, *But you're a very good worker, Suzy, I can't understand that.* I had to reposition Suzy's foot a few times to get it believable. I raised the boss's hand in an expressive flutter as he said the phrase.

Happy with that, I moved to the next panel and sketched

the same scene yet again. I had overlays that I could choose from: Suzy's desk, her usual clothing, the boss's suit, parts of the characters in various expressions, but they were still buried in one of the unpacked boxes beneath the worktable. This strip would be totally freehand, and I was actually enjoying the process. It made it seem less like production and more like the art it had begun as.

Engrossed in my work, I absently reached up and patted Oscar Marie's overhanging paw when she moved restlessly. She mewed, but it wasn't comfort.

I glanced up and saw that she was looking at something behind me. My gaze flew to the darkened windowpane. I saw reflected behind me and to the right, just over my shoulder, a thin pale woman with long black hair.

I screamed, unable to help myself. She dissipated like morning fog. I whirled, trying in vain to catch my breath, but there was no one there. Gasping for air, my heart hammering in my chest like it would burst any second, I stood. After grasping my high stool for support, I backed away from the center of the room until my back was against the wall. Oscar Marie watched me calmly, her tail twitching.

My thoughts raced as frantically as my heart. Mary's hair had been shorter, her face not as narrow. I tried to picture the woman again. Her eyes, milky white in the centers, had been outlined in black. A shudder raced through me as I saw those eyes once more in my mind. Pushing the image away, I allowed my gaze to roam the room while my heart slowed and I could breathe again. I remained standing in my protected stance, however.

Obviously, this building was haunted. I still believed it was Mary, wanted it to be her. But what if it wasn't? I wondered suddenly if there was a history of haunting here. I mean with a cemetery so close…suppose Ruetta knew about the ghost? If so, why hadn't Maddy warned me? And the most important question: would this unknown spirit really hurt me or Oscar Marie?

ANGIE

"Wow, that's weird," I said, tucking my order pad back into my apron pocket.

"We don't usually have storms this early in the year," Cosgrove said.

I turned my gaze from the television mounted high on the wall above the bar and examined him. He looked good today, dressed uncharacteristically in a suit and tie with his balding pate hatless and what remained of his hair combed neatly. I hadn't had a chance to say hello to him this morning because Gail was working the bar.

"Look at you, all dressed up! What's going on?" I asked.

"Oh, gotta speak to the gang today." His already ruddy skin darkened a bit. "They require it. Trying to better themselves, I guess."

I smiled. Cosgrove was on the board of the Port Isabel Fisherman's Collective, a group dedicated to improving the plight of the local shrimpers and commercial fishermen. They also did a lot of solid charitable work. An idea popped into my head.

"So what projects do you guys have going on over there right now?" I took his discarded breakfast plate and moved to the back of the bar to place it in one of the bus bins.

He shrugged and took another swig of his coffee. "Nothing right now. We finished everything from last year and our new projects start next month with our fiscal year. Why?"

I took a quick glance at the three tables of diners I was caring for today. Seeing that they seemed content, I briefly explained the SPICEY dilemma to him.

"Man, Ange, that's just harsh," he said sympathetically with a grimace on his weathered, but newly shaven face. He paused to think. "You know, we probably can't save the building, but we might be able to do some fundraising to get you guys settled someplace else. I'll see what I can do. Maybe someone today will know of an empty place. I'll ask around."

"Oh, man, you are too cool. Thank you," I told him. I wanted to sweep around the bar and give him a big hug, but for some reason I was feeling a bit raw today so I held back.

"No problem, kiddo." He motioned toward the television with his cup. "What's the deal with the weather?"

I glanced up and saw that the national weather of the morning talk show had been replaced by news commentary. "Looks like it's coming from the west. They're not sure how low it will dip down though." I grabbed the coffee carafe and refilled his cup, wondering what had happened to Gail.

"You remember that one about four years ago? Took down trees, that one did, and that was nigh onto the end of March."

I laughed, remembering the scary time. "Do I ever. I thought we were going to have a restaurant full of spring breakers sleeping on the floor here."

"And me too," Sanchez piped up, lifting her face from the Tamaulipas newspaper she had been reading. "There was no way I was driving home in that mess."

"Oh, right, flooding on the island. I remember that." Cosgrove added sugar to his cup. "I sure hope we don't have that craziness again."

"What craziness?" asked Ernie Henson as he took a barstool next to Cosgrove.

The two men shook hands. Ernie waved politely to Sanchez.

"Storm coming," Cosgrove explained. "Early."

"Coffee, Ernie?" I held up a mug. At his nod, I placed the mug in front of him and filled it. I pushed the bowl of individual creamers and the sugar toward him, and then leaned over to freshen Anna's cup.

"Wheat toast and two scrambled," he said.

I jotted it down on the back of my pad as I went into the kitchen to find Gail.

I found Gail and Mama huddled around the toaster-sized kitchen television.

"What in the world are ya'll doing?" I asked.

"Storm's coming," Gail said.

"Yeah, I saw," I said. "Listen, you have four at the bar now. Ernie just came in." I turned to Mama. "Wheat and two scrambled," I told her before heading out to take care of my tables.

I was checking out the last of the morning rush when Grey stepped into the restaurant. I was so happy to see her! I rushed forward and hugged her close, and that was when I realized how terrified she was. I pulled back and examined her. She looked as though she hadn't slept in days. Dark circles had taken up residence right below those beautiful green eyes.

"What in the world?" I asked. I pulled her into a side alcove before she could answer and placed her carefully in one of the chairs. "Stay here." I ordered.

I moved behind the bar and stuck my head into the kitchen. "I'm on break, Mama," I said. "No tables and Gail's got the bar."

I asked Gail to watch for new customers as I poured out two cups of coffee and dropped a handful of creamers into my apron pocket.

Grey was where I had left her, her chin in her palm, looking waiflike in her misery.

"Here," I said setting the coffee before her. "Basics first."

I slid into the chair opposite her and slammed the handful of creamer on the table. The little plastic canisters rolled. Grey caught one before it rolled off the table.

"I always get the best service when I come here," she joked.

I made a face at her and sipped my coffee black, enjoying the mellowness after Mama's penchant for harsh chicory coffee when I was growing up. "So what's going on?"

"I need you to come stay with me."

I lifted my eyebrows in surprise and swallowed a mouthful of coffee.

She sighed and closed her eyes. "Wait. Let me do that again. I was just talking to Maddy and she says you're like a…a psychic for hire, right?"

I nodded slowly, totally bemused by the conversation.

"Well, I want to hire you." She poured a trio of creamers into her coffee. Unwrapping a setup, she stirred diligently with a spoon and placed the paper napkin daintily in her lap.

"Hire me?" This wasn't exactly what I had envisioned.

"Yes, and I don't care what it costs."

A flare went off in my mind. I thought of what it would cost to pay for the security deposit on a new facility for the SPICEY. Maybe this was the answer come knocking.

"Well, why don't you tell me what's going on?"

GREY

I saw dawn creep into my bedroom with jaundiced eyes. I had tried to sleep, tried hard, but every time I closed my eyes and drifted off, I would hear the voice talking to me. Sometimes the female voice whispered endearments which warmed me. Other times, she wept as if her heart were breaking. I answered back, but it seemed like Mary—or whoever the ghost was—just ignored me.

I'd left my bedroom lamp on to allay my fear. Poor Oscar Marie huddled next to me, her eyes wide as activity whirled around us. Once I nodded off, but was jerked to full awareness when *Abandoned*, that ever prevalent book of poems, dropped on my blanketed feet. I waited a few cautious minutes before quickly retrieving it. I opened the book, hoping for answers. A sudden thought occurred to me.

"Annalise? Is that you?" I whispered to the empty room. A sudden wind swept through the room, bearing a faint wail, and then I felt the entity leave me alone. Now, if it *was* Mary, had I made her jealous? I couldn't win in this situation, it seemed. I lifted the book.

> *Buddha belly*
> *would accept you in*
> *and keep you safe*
> *As I rage against injustice*
> *Lulling there like*
> *A horse dream*
> *Mellow and warm*
>
> *And by born*
> *You rip me anew*
> *And my feet are wet*
> *Blood or tears*
> *Friend of fears*
> *Buddha wept*

I turned the book over and read the brief blurb about the life of poet Eleanor Copeland. She was called a Beat poet and could be seen performing live at The Gotham in Midtown as well as The Nip in Bryant Park. Sort of cryptic.

I opened the front cover and noted that the publishing company was called the Independent Press of Columbia University. I flipped to the dedication page. *To my darling Annalise, love and righteousness forever.* To say I was confused would be an understatement. What did a Beat poet from New York City have to do with a South Texas fishing village?

He promised us
The world
The California
Coastline boastline
Will you go?
Farewell
the last sigh
from your lips
cherry dark
fruited
Abandoned
Love chain broken
Battered
Pain numbed
Ingrained into texture
Never abandoned

I placed the book carefully on the small table next to the bed and caressed Oscar Marie as I waited for the promised protection of daylight. I thought about leaving. There was a hotel further inland. It just seemed like running yet again. And suppose it was Mary trapped here somehow? Leaving her when she might be trying to talk to me would be the ultimate betrayal.

For some odd reason, my thoughts flew to Angie. I wondered at the mystery of her life. She worked two jobs, it seemed, delivering pizzas and teaching special needs kids. I wondered about her family and her relationships, wishing I'd had more opportunity to talk with her while we were in Couscous's busy kitchen.

I finally dozed, feeling as though her serene blue gaze protected me.

I was pondering my chores for the day when a cheery knock sounded on the kitchen door. I nearly jumped out of my skin, of course, but hurried to lift the curtain and peer through the glass top of the door. Maddy stood on the decking outside. Today, her jogging suit was pale pink with white stripes in symmetrical patterns. When I opened the door, the sun shone off her new athletic shoes, blazing up at me.

"Well, good morning, stranger!" Maddy said. "I just thought I'd drop by and see how our newest resident is settling in." She handed me a plastic wrapped bundle: a fragrant cinnamon coffee cake, still warm from the oven.

"Whoa! Thank you!" I was touched by her thoughtfulness. "Come have some with me?"

"Don't mind if I do," she said, stepping into the kitchen.

"I actually have dishes now."

"Well, I would say that's progress," she murmured as she came in and meandered over to the drafting table. "Oh, this must be your cartoon! I can't believe you sit here and draw this, and it just magically appears in all those magazines and newspapers."

"Yep. If it gets there. It's been slow going this week," I replied with a weary sigh. I poured coffee into two cups and added them to a serving tray along with sugar, milk, and the coffee cake. I included plates and utensils and carried the tray to the table.

"Why is that?" Her brow furrowed in confusion. "Too busy settling in?"

"No, not exactly." I sat down and served slices of the cake. I hesitated, but made up my mind quickly. "Let me ask you this: did Ruetta ever say anything about weird things happening here?"

Maddy prepared her coffee thoughtfully. "Weird? Weird, how?"

I shrugged, trying to sound more nonchalant than I felt. "Like things moving...weird sounds?"

"Hmm." Maddy sat back in her chair. "I don't remember her saying anything like that. Why do you ask?"

I debated how much to tell her. I didn't want to be labeled a lunatic in my first few weeks in my new home. Yet I felt a deep curiosity that I couldn't shake and I needed to ask questions. "I've been hearing some noises during the night."

"Oh, that's probably just being in a new place," she said, taking a bite of the cake. "Especially here. Tourist towns are notoriously busy, even into the wee hours."

I shook my head. "Nope. It's inside. I've seen things move as well. I know it sounds a little crazy…"

"Well, not crazy, but I'm sure there's a logical explanation. What has been happening?"

How could I summarize the events of the past few nights into something she would easily understand without sounding like I was trying to craft a script for a bad horror movie? I sighed and started sharing some of the things I'd experienced. I tried to keep it light, but I know it all sounded unbelievable. I told her so, shaking my head apologetically.

"Well, now, if it's real to you, then that makes it an issue for sure." She scratched her chin absently. "Have you tried talking to this…ghost?"

"Well, yeah." I rose and brought the carafe over to refill our cups. "I've tried, but don't get any sort of answer. It's all kind of… disconnected, you know?"

"Sounds like you need a medium."

I resumed my seat. "Like with the turban and the crystal ball? I don't know. Seems too weird."

Maddy shrugged. "No weirder than what you are dealing with, I'm thinking."

We sat in silence for almost a minute, both of us lost in thought.

"How does one go about getting a medium?" I asked finally.

"I was just thinking that myself," she replied with a short laugh. "I do know of one woman here in The Point, a psychic. The police hire her from time to time."

"Really?" I leaned toward her eagerly. "Do you think she would help me get to the bottom of the whole thing?"

Maddy stood. "It wouldn't hurt you to ask. All she can say is no and then you'd just be back at square one."

"Will you give me her number? I don't know if I'll call but…"

Maddy smiled and fished her car keys out of her pocket, preparing to head out. "Better yet, I'll tell you where to find her."

ANGIE

I listened to Grey talk about being haunted and found myself watching her instead. The way her hands moved as she formed words and thoughts, the way her eyes darkened or lightened when she relived the events, and the sweet way her hair parted over her ears when she tucked it back behind them. I was so smitten with her.

"You've been having a horrible time," I said softly when her story ran down. "Of course I will help you."

"So you'll come stay?"

"The night?" I shook my head. "I don't know. I could probably just come by and..."

"Please? I...I will pay you for your time." Her embarrassment was evident. I sensed her desperation and her fear. "Maybe just the weekend?"

Agonizing with myself because I would have helped her for free, I thought of the children. I thought of Maria and the feel of a knife at my throat. I suddenly knew I could ask.

"I'm...I'm expensive," I said, knowing that my cheeks were growing pink. "But I will guarantee I will get to the bottom of the situation for you. I *will* take care of it."

She eyed me doubtfully. Who could blame her? Those who truly get information by occult means have been irreparably harmed by those using subterfuge and false get-rich-quick schemes for profit. I was not proud of myself, but knew I had to find a new home for the SPICEY kids.

"And?" she prompted.

I swallowed hard. "Two thousand dollars."

Her eyes widened. I watched her face change, grow hard, and I almost recanted, told her I didn't mean it. Pride and need stayed my voice, and then it was too late. She stood and slowly placed her napkin on the table, her expression a mask of coolness.

"Well, I see I've made a mistake," she said with a sigh. She turned and walked out of the restaurant.

I almost ran after her. I did run to the door, but was waylaid by an influx of regulars coming in for the lunch special. I watched her walk away and my heart was crushed. I worried that I had lost her for good, but I vowed to go to her that evening after work. To explain the situation and beg her forgiveness.

I left The Fat Mother at one o'clock and taught my usual classes at the SPICEY, but my heart wasn't in it. I suddenly knew a sense of loss such as I'd never experienced before. How could I have been so stupid as to push away the best thing that had ever happened to me? Pushed it away even before it could have manifested into the positive event I felt it could be.

After helping load the kids into the van for their ride home, I jumped into my Jeep and drove to work my night shift at the restaurant.

"Hey, Mama," I said, walking into the kitchen through the back door. She stood at the dough board, working.

"Hey, baby." She glanced at the clock high up on the kitchen wall. "You're early."

I grabbed a bowl and helped myself to some of the roasted redskin potatoes still steaming on the warming table. "Yeah, I got a problem and need to get off early, if that's okay."

She was kneading the pizza dough. As I munched potatoes, I watched her. She really was a good cook. Her powerful body just seemed naturally to know the best way to move as she pushed and pulled the large wad of dough. It was a gift. She managed a restaurant well too.

I studied the kitchen and saw the usual offerings were all ready to go. Huge pots of fragrant sauces simmered on the stove, and warming bins of pasta and the vegetables of the day waited. The pizza *sous* bins were full of toppings and the dough backups looked good.

Finishing the kneading, she plopped the dough into one of the waiting bowls, covered it, and wiped her hands on a kitchen towel.

"Only if you talk to me." Mama studied me with curiosity, her gaze level and insistent.

"Grey wants me to check out her new place. She thinks it's haunted." I set the potatoes aside, wondering how much Mama would get out of me.

"Well, that's fantastic—" She broke off and looked at me again. "And that's a problem, because..."

I sighed and leaned against the oven wall. "She offered to pay."

"And that's a problem, because..." she repeated, starting to frown.

"I told her a couple thousand..."

"You what? Why on earth…Angela Rose, what were you thinking?"

"It's for SPICEY, Mama. To get the money for a down payment." I hated the whiney tone that had infiltrated my voice.

"Now, Angie, I told you that would all work out. We're gonna juggle the money here at the restaurant, call in some favors. I told you I would go to the next council meeting."

"Mama, like I said, I am not going to have you fighting my battles for me. I saw Frankee the other day, and she won't budge and we're just out of time. We have less than a month now."

"That doesn't make gouging that girl the right thing to do."

I groaned and held my head with both hands. "I know, Mama! I know, for Pete's sake."

"Well, you just need to get on over there and tell her you were being a fool."

I set my jaw hard. "I plan to, Mama. Tonight after work. That's why I need to get off a little early."

"No problem. I can handle cleanup on my own. Maybe I'll ask Gail to stay a little later than nine."

"Who will be here 'til closing?" I didn't want Mama in the restaurant alone until eleven at night.

"Hasty. And I can fit in that Peterson girl. She's been looking for extra hours." Mama reached up to the carousel and peered at her next order even as I descended on her in a bear hug.

Holding her close, I leaned my head back and studied her sweet face. "You is the bestest muvver evah."

She blushed and pecked a kiss on the end of my nose. "You and me against the world, baby girl."

I held her a moment longer, just because I could. "I have potato breath," I told her.

"I know," she responded deadpan. "We need a Pasta Bolognese on table three."

I released her and grabbed an apron. "Consider it done, oh great mother of mine."

GREY

I slammed shut the front door of the Bookmark and looked around carefully to make sure nothing had magically changed while I was away. Finding all as it should be, I went ahead and locked the door, even setting the alarm. I would not be going out again until the strip was finished. No matter how much my elusive ghostie tried to frighten me.

I knew I was still too angry to work on the strip properly, so I moved behind the coffee counter and began unpacking one of the four coffeemakers I had purchased on my trip into Brownsville. I needed physical labor to deal with my irate mood.

Imagine her wanting to charge me that outrageous amount just for helping me out by doing her mystical woo-woo thing for me. I value a job well done and would have paid a lot. Five hundred, even a thousand, maybe, but two thousand dollars? That was just too much. I could feel myself seething in anger as I methodically placed items on the counter. I didn't need her help. I would handle this issue just fine by myself.

I stopped what I was doing, afraid I would start tossing coffee cups against the far wall, and began pacing to and fro down the middle of the Bookmark. I had actually believed that she was someone special. Someone I could have an interest in once I got over the loss of Mary. I had a sudden image of her with Vetty's baby. I remembered her with her students on the beach. I felt her warming, firm hug.

I growled in outrage and opened the door to my apartment. This kind of mental volleyball was getting me nowhere fast. I had a strip due, a time-consuming freehand one, and I simply had to focus on that.

Oscar Marie opened an eye and watched me from her perch on the back of the sofa. She yawned dramatically and stretched each leg as she made her way down to the floor.

"I'm glad some of us can sleep," I told her sarcastically as I perched on my stool.

Oscar Marie ignored me and slid as gracefully as any runway model across the floor and into the kitchen to nibble daintily at the tidbits in her bowl.

I studied the strip, trying to psyche myself up into working on it. I picked up a marker and slammed it down again. Angie had some nerve, making me care for her. I cupped my chin in my hand and looked out at the sage-blue water of the bay.

I saw the island off in the distance. A huge part of me wanted to go there, bury my feet in the sand, and stay the rest of my life. I wanted to let go of responsibility, let go of caring.

Unfortunately, I did care. About work anyway, and I would not miss this deadline.

Taking a deep breath, I lifted the smaller marker. The next panel was a repeat of the one following it. Suzy sat behind the desk. Mister Marks was in the same chair with his feet on the desk, a cigar in his mouth. They were both talking in this panel. Mister Marks said, *Ah, yes, receptionist for that financial firm downtown*, and Suzy replied, *Yes, sir, that's the one.*

I sketched carefully, my hands following well-worn paths. I moved Mister Marks's cigar to his right hand as he punctuated his memory of where she had worked before. I drew a single line denoting smoke from the ash end of the cigar. Suzy lifted the sheet of paper she would be examining in the next panel. Both her feet were on the ground and she was slanted forward.

Finished with her meal, Oscar Marie decided to join me and leapt up to perch on her observation platform. I gave her a quick scratch around the scruff of her neck.

Feeling good about what I had accomplished, I began on the preceding panel. Again, I sketched the mundane framework. Suzy was digging in an overlarge handbag in this one. After drawing it in, I quickly sketched the same handbag into the following three panels. Props could make or break a strip. I placed the handbag on the floor against the side of the desk that faced the reader to add some nice visual interest.

I was denied a raise at my other job, sir. The phrase hovered above Suzy's head. Mister Marks puffed on his cigar, his cheeks bellowed out a little. His curved fingers appeared to be twirling the cylinder in his mouth.

The final panel waited. *I'm not 100 % sure why you came to Marks & Crocker, Suzy.* The text was on the left in this panel, behind the boss's balding head. I sketched the character carefully, using my ruler to make sure there would be enough room. Suzy looked at Mister Marks as he spoke this time. Her expression was one of pure forbearance, as if she couldn't believe the man was actually talking to her and wasting her time. I smiled. Yep, that was Suzy.

At last, the fundamentals were finished. Now all it needed was the overall shading and the walls of the office in the background drawn in. I rose and stretched my arms over my head. I looked around, suddenly feeling as though I were being watched.

"Mary? Is that you?" I called out.

I looked at Oscar Marie. She was not reacting so I laughed nervously and chalked the feeling up to an overactive imagination. The haunting of the past few days seemed like a dream during normal, calm times.

Now that I had come to a stopping point, I realized anew how extremely tired I felt. No wonder I imagined new daytime hauntings as well as dealing with the real nighttime phenomena.

The deck outside beckoned so I pulled open the back door and was inundated with hot ocean wind. I breathed deeply of the salt air, feeling revitalized. I waved to Oscar Marie and stepped outside, shutting the door behind me.

I stood at the railing a good while, enjoying the poetry of the Laguna Madre, the Mother Lagoon. I had read that Laguna Madre was home to more finfish than any other place on the Texas coast, making it a boon for recreational as well as commercial fishermen. It was saltier than the ocean on the other side of Padre Island due to an almost nonexistent exchange rate.

All I knew for sure was that the scenery of the self-contained lagoon was incredible. As the time was approaching late afternoon, huge spills of pink, cotton candy clouds sprawled across the horizon. I saw the lowering sun off to my left, and though it was still early, I felt a sense of settling in for the night.

The shallows of the strip of water separating the island from the mainland were the home ground to a huge assortment of land and waterfowl such as brown and white pelicans, egrets and gulls galore. Ducks were a constant presence in the calm backwaters as well. I loved their little chuckling sounds that carried to me on the wind.

I took a seat on one of the two Adirondack chairs and relaxed. I stared at the dusky sky and thought about Angie. I felt sad that I would no longer be able to get to know her. If I faced my feelings honestly, my new loneliness, I realized I had been looking forward to cultivating a friendship with her. Or maybe something more. But I also knew that no matter how lonely and misplaced I felt, I had no room in my life for friends who tried to take advantage of me.

I closed my eyes and pictured her. She was so beautiful and seemed so even-tempered. I remembered her sense of humor and smiled to myself. I was angry with her, true, and understood she was gone from my life as a love interest, but at the same time, all I could see was her smile and the warmth shining from her deep blue eyes.

ANGIE

I peered through the front doors of Grey's coffee shop. The thick glass was hard to see through, but I saw no light evident anywhere. I strode around the street side and down a small incline, following the sidewalk to the back of the building, a bag with some of Mama's good cooking in it banging against my thighs.

The concrete sidewalk ended and turned into a wooden walkway that passed behind the building. I mounted a few steps and there, childlike and beautiful in the gentle glow of the condo streetlights along the water, lay Grey curled in a chair, cuddled into herself, her arms wrapped around her knees.

I sat on the steps and watched her a long time, the slap of the tide loud in my ears. I hated to disturb her because she was sleeping so peacefully, but I also knew that nights on the water chilled quickly.

I moved closer and knelt next to the chair. I had picked up a handful of apology flowers from Estella's shop and I used them now to gently tickle Grey's chin. She stirred, then woke suddenly. Her first reaction was to smile, but then I suppose she remembered the foolishness of the morning and her face closed to me.

"Good morning, sunshine," I said, determined to charm her into a new mindset. "You looked pretty comfy there."

She sat up, as if annoyed that I had seen her in such a vulnerable position. "I must have dozed off," she murmured.

"Can we go inside? I just want to talk with you a minute."

She scrubbed her palms on her thighs as if undecided, but finally agreed, and we moved into the kitchen. I walked in behind Grey and slammed bodily into her when she abruptly stopped.

A low moan sounded. I wasn't sure at first where it came from, but when I touched Grey's bare arm to keep myself from stumbling, sheer abject terror washed through me. I peered over Grey's shoulder and was amazed to see that, over to the left, every cabinet door and drawer in the kitchen gaped open. It was a bizarre sight.

"Did you leave it this way?" I whispered, already knowing the answer. I moved further into the dining room to gain a better vantage point.

It was amazing. Each open door of each top cabinet was lined up with unbelievable vertical precision to the one below it. In addition, each drawer was open the exact same amount as the one above and below. I'd never seen anything like it.

I leaned to close the door to outside while Grey stood as if shell-shocked. I shifted her to a nearby easy chair and moved into the kitchen to start closing cabinets and drawers until normalcy was restored.

I glared at the cabinets, just daring them to open again as I moved back to Grey's side. I caught movement out of the corner of my eye and saw a large furry cat, jet-black with huge green eyes, perched on the drafting board that dominated the dining room.

I glanced at Grey. "And who is this?" I asked, indicating the cat. I moved closer and extended my hand so the cat could smell me. He was friendly and butted my hand, seeking affection.

"Her name is Oscar Marie," Grey said quietly.

"Well, hello, Oscar Marie," I cooed, scratching her ears. I was trying to avoid talking about the issue with the cabinets. I looked down.

"What's this?" I asked, lifting the thick sheet of paper. "Do you draw cartoons? I've seen this one, this Sassy Suzy, in our local paper. Oh, my God, don't tell me, you're *that* Graham?"

Grey nodded and lifted her eyes. Suddenly, she was on her feet, taking the paper from my hands. "No," she wailed. "Oh, no!" She took a step back, the paper still held in her hands. She fell into the chair she'd just left, tears welling in her eyes.

"Why is she doing this to me?" she whispered, asking the question of me.

I had no answer, but I was brokenhearted by her tone. I moved close to her. "Who? Mary? What is she doing?"

She held the overlarge sheet out to me. I took it doubtfully, afraid of what I would see.

"What? It looks…"

"Panel three," she said in a monotone of pain. "I didn't do that."

I looked at the third square. There was a man on the left and a bored looking secretary on the right. Sassy Suzy and her boss.

Then I saw it. On each side there were phrases printed neatly in capital letters formed into a box format but between them, scribbled haphazardly in black marker was a poem of some kind. I read it aloud.

My Anna
You are
abandoned
Forgive my lie

My love lives on
Yet I weep

My world is
Darkened
Without your
smile

I looked at her. "So who do you think did this, Grey? The ghost you told me about? Or Mary? This is so cryptic…it makes no sense."

"They never do, really," she said dully. "I can't believe I have to do that panel again! And it's due on Monday."

I could tell she was near her breaking point so I quickly replaced the comic strip on the table and knelt beside her. I looked into her eyes, making her see me. "We'll take care of this," I told her. "*I* will take care of this."

She pulled her gaze away, nodded, then sighed loudly. "Okay," she said. "Okay."

I glanced toward the kitchen and saw the flowers I had put on the counter. I suddenly remembered the food Mama had shoved into my hands. "Listen, I brought dinner. Let's get some food in us and we'll plan a strategy, okay?"

GREY

I thought my heart would stop beating when I saw what Mary had done to my strip. She, of all people, knew what my work meant to me. But then that may have been why she chose that particular point of attack. But why was she mad at me? I wasn't responsible for her death. It had to be because I sold our home and moved. Guilt raged in me.

Being with Angie filled me with a tempest of mixed emotions as well. On the one hand, I definitely needed her with me. On the other, I was still furious at her for trying to make such a huge profit out of my distress.

Seeing the apartment and my life violated, so openly and completely, placed me into a uniquely vulnerable position. I felt I needed Angie to resolve it. I couldn't continue living this way. My sanity and now my work was suffering because of the relentless assaults. So I would pay her fee. I had little choice.

I studied her as she worked the microwave and prepared dinner for us. Her expression was thoughtful and she was fully engrossed in her task. She looked so cute in her baggy cargo shorts and retro cut T-shirt.

She had taken her hair down. It surrounded her head in an unruly lion's mane reaching to her shoulders.

I studied her forearms when she retrieved the dish of pasta. Her arms and shoulders were so powerful. I had felt the extent of that power when she hugged me on the beach. I suddenly realized that I wanted more of those hugs, but scowled and pushed that thought away. Angie might be getting my money, but that was all. We had a business arrangement. I would not make the mistake of believing we were friends.

"Here we go," she said, carrying the bowl to the table and placing it on a hot pad. "Some of Mama's finest, her stuffed manicotti." She paused to adjust one of the flowers she had arranged into a vase earlier.

"It looks delicious," I murmured, the sight and smell making my stomach gurgle in anticipatory delight.

She brought back a bowl of veggie peppered tossed salad and a trio of hot buttered rolls. I was lost in a gustatory dreamland and my mouth began to water.

"Can we open this wine?" She held up a bottle of Malbec I'd left on the counter.

"Of course," I said. Soon, a glass stood before me. I took a long, necessary drink and enjoyed the spicy heat as the wine traveled to my stomach. I covered my eyes with both hands, willing normalcy to return. I felt Angie slide into the seat across from me.

"So you're Graham, the controversial lesbian cartoonist." Angie made it a statement. "I had no idea."

I sat back and looked at her. "That would be me."

She took my plate and served me a portion of the manicotti and a heaping serving spoonful of salad. "It's already dressed with Mama's oil and vinegar herb mix. Hope you like it."

I tasted it. A perfect blend. "It's wonderful," I said.

"So how does one become a cartoonist?" Angie asked, as I had expected.

"Pure luck. And some connections made at the UTD art program." I tasted the manicotti, finding it so well prepared that it melted into simple richness in my mouth.

"Were you always interested in comic strips?" She offered me the saucer of warm rolls and I took one.

"Yeah, pretty much. I read a lot of comic books and loved the movement and the colors. Then I started scribbling on my own, copying from them into my notebooks. It…it kind of became an obsession."

"One that panned out for you in a big way," Angie said. Her smile was warm and endearing. I hated the verbal reminder of her evident greed. I looked away.

"And now you are syndicated. That must feel pretty good."

"It's just a job. Like waiting tables."

I saw her frown slightly as my subtle jibe hit home. I decided it was probably better to get to the subject at hand so I could be rid of her as quickly as possible.

"So you've seen what this…force here is doing. Do you think you can drive it away?"

Angie placed her fork next to her plate and entwined her hands together in front of her chin. "I really don't know. Most of the time, I just find people who are dead and their bodies are missing. I've never dealt with a haunting like this before."

"How will you proceed?" I felt new doubt swell in me.

"Usually I touch something that the person I'm looking for has used on a regular basis."

I leapt to my feet. "I have one of Mary's shirts—" I began only to be cut off by Angie's low whistle.

"Dinner first, Grey. We'll need our energy."

I sat reluctantly, peeved that I was forced to sit with her. She must have sensed my reluctance since her good mood seemed to dissipate.

"Tell me about the books again."

I told her about the floating tornado of books and how they had been thrown at me.

"I think I'll spend the night in the book room, see what energies I can pick up there. I'll want to have a look at that little book you told me about too. See what info I can glean from it."

"Sure. It's in the bedroom."

She cocked an eyebrow at me. "Why the bedroom?"

I shrugged. "Mary did it, not me. For some reason, she keeps forcing this book of poems on me and I have no idea why. It's not even one we discussed when she was alive. It's a complete mystery to me."

"Poetry?"

"Yeah, like what was on the strip. Weird, non-rhyming stuff. Very obscure." I pushed my plate away. I'd had enough of the excellent food.

Angie sat back in her seat and took a leisurely drink of her wine, twirling the glass when finished. I noted the sure way her fingers gripped the stem. Her nails were short and well cared for, even buffed shiny.

"So tell me this: why do you think Mary is haunting you? Did you have a good or a troubled relationship?"

I resented her question and hoped my level gaze told her so. "It was good."

"Why plague you with poltergeist activity? Try to hurt you?"

"Now that's the question of the day," I said, hoping she got my sarcasm. I stood and started clearing the table. She stood to help.

"Maybe it's not Mary," she suggested.

"I thought of that." I placed the scraped dishes in the sink and looked out the window at the darkened bay. "The woman I saw in the window that evening didn't really look like her. So I asked Maddy if the place had been haunted before I moved in and she said no." I looked at Angie. "So it has to be Mary. Who else could it be?"

"Well, that's what I am here for," she said with a sigh as she moved to help me with the dishes.

I stopped her. "I'm fine here." I pulled my hands away, enjoying the feel of her skin too much. "Why don't you go into the Bookmark and have a look around?"

She looked at my hands as I lifted a dishtowel.

"I'll do that. You sure you're okay here?"

I nodded. She handed me the serving bowl of pasta she'd brought from the table, and walked out of the kitchen.

ANGIE

There's something about the smell of paper, ink and glue that is endemic to all libraries, and in this case, a reading room. I guess any place where a large number of books are assembled. I smelled the not unpleasant odor as soon as I stepped into the attractive, comfortable space.

The artfully arranged furniture had brought a sense of coziness to the large, high-ceilinged room. I was impressed by Grey's good taste. I walked to one of the small windows set into the side wall and saw a good view of The Fat Mother and the other businesses along that arm of Lighthouse Square, like Estella's Flowers and More, Maxwell's Pub, and Penny's Ice Cream Hut. It was definitely weird seeing all of them from this vantage point.

I suddenly felt a presence behind me so I straightened my back and opened to it. My opening must have confused or frightened the entity because it vanished almost immediately. I turned, and as expected, saw nothing.

There was someone here. I knew that now, having felt her. I hadn't picked up a name but I had felt her presence. She was artistic and sorrowful, but I picked up little beyond that. If only she hadn't been spooked—I cringed inwardly at the inadvertent pun—I could have discovered more, like what she hoped to gain by haunting Grey.

I wrapped both arms around myself as I strolled through the reading room. I stepped into the other part and saw a couple of heavy brocade lounge chairs. Two library tables with comfy rolling chairs were toward the front, below the windows that fronted on the street.

A wide side door was set on the east wall at the back of the room. By peering through the large windows set in that same wall, I saw that the door opened onto an alley between Grey's place and the art collective next door.

I walked back into the main room and envisioned it full of readers enjoying coffee served from the two counters on each side in the back. I thought it a great innovative idea for The Point. I'd been to a few reading rooms and loved the relaxed, erudite conversations they engendered.

I sighed as I opened the door to the apartment. It would be a good addition to the area provided I could get to the bottom of this haunting.

Grey was finishing up in the kitchen. The food had been put away, and our few dishes washed and left air drying in the dish drainer.

"It all looks quiet in there," I informed her.

"Good. So what do we do now?" She handed me another glass of wine.

I nodded my thanks. "Now we just wait for something to happen. Can you get me the book that seems to be the catalyst?"

She nodded and stepped into a hallway next to the kitchen.

I heard her gasp as soon as the light clicked on. I placed my glass down on the counter, sensing trouble.

"Leave my things alone!" she shrieked even as I raced down the hall.

Another strange sight met my gaze. I stopped in the doorway and sighed. The restless spirit had been at it again. The large bed was covered with clothing, obviously Grey's, and it had been arranged in a series of neat piles, sorted by color.

"I'm guessing it's not laundry day?" I asked.

Grey turned her angry gaze on me. "You think?"

She stepped to the nightstand and picked up a small book. She slammed it into my belly and shoved me out the door.

"Just do your damned work and leave me be," she said, pushing the door shut.

I stared at the closed door for almost a minute, the book clutched to my body. She was fierce when riled. I almost felt sorry for the ghost of Mary.

Oscar Marie watched me with cool disinterest when I entered the living room. I switched on the lamp next to a Queen Anne chair against the wall and took a seat.

"Looks like it's just you and me, Oscar Mayer," I told the cat as I settled in and opened the small volume, a collection of poems by a woman named Eleanor Copeland.

By glancing through the poetry, I figured out she was one of the Beat poets of the late forties or early fifties. I tapped the book on my chin, pondering. What did this book have to do with the haunting? I stilled as a sudden image formed in my mind.

She was a slim, pale woman with a thick shock of red hair and soft blue eyes, thickly outlined with black liner. She smiled. I saw that her prominent outer incisors curved inward, giving her a distinctive, impish grin. She faced away from me, but looked back to laugh at me as the wind blew hair across her face. She was young and beautiful, and I loved her. *My Annalise...*

I shook my head to clear it even as I realized I was freezing. It was a bone-chilling cold, clammy and distasteful. About the same time, I realized the temperature had dropped. I also realized that I could no longer breathe.

Cold, hard fingers were clenched so tightly around my throat that no air could get past them. I panicked, intensely confused, and afraid. My body reacted instinctively, thrashing to escape the deadly pressure around my windpipe. I pushed out against thin air, but it did no good. The fingers were relentless. My heels pounded the wooden floor. I finally used my elbows to try and rise from the chair, anything to escape the heavy weight crushing me.

Light slanted across the room. I spied Grey racing toward me from the bedroom. She was screaming angrily as she grabbed my arms and pulled me from the chair. Only then did the frigid weight move off me. The fingers loosened around my windpipe. Gasping for air, I fell to the floor, whimpering in pain. My throat felt raw and heated now that the coldness had fled.

"Oh, my God, Angie, please tell me you're okay. Please..." Grey knelt beside me.

I waved my hand at her to let her know I would be all right if I could just catch a full breath and ease the pain in my throat. I tried to rise and she leapt to help me.

When I gained my feet, I heard her gasp. "Oh, Angie, your neck."

I wanted to ask her what was wrong, but my voice was a sad croak. She stared at my neck and reached out a hand to touch the area. I touched her arm, opened to her, and saw that my neck was scratched, with red welts and purple bruises already appearing. I was going to have a lot of fun explaining that to Mama.

"Let me get you some ice to put on that," Grey said.

I shook my head. I'd had just about enough cold for one night.

GREY

I watched Angie as she slept in my bed, Oscar Marie curled next to her. Angie was so beautiful and the brutal welts and bruises on the delicate skin of her neck made my heart hurt for her. I was also terrified.

I had figured, perhaps expected, that a ghost was too vaporous to do physical damage. That their damage consisted of the psychological terror they caused by catching us off guard. But here was Angie, bearing the actual marks of a spectral attack. I didn't know how to file that away and make it innocuous.

I glanced down the hallway into the brightly lit living room. There would be no way I would turn off all the lights at night ever again.

All was quiet right now, though, and I was grateful for that. I had cleaned off the bed, putting my clothing back into the covered bins at the foot end. I was so glad that I had finished when I had, or Angie might have been hurt even more seriously.

I sure was getting tired of neatening up after this bothersome spirit. I thought of the Suzy panel, knowing I would have to fix that in the morning.

The unfairness of Mary ruining the panel paled in comparison to her hurting Angie. I looked at the sleeping woman again. She stirred restlessly. I laid a calming hand on her leg where it rested beneath the comforter. She whispered my name in her wounded, croaking voice, and I looked at her to make sure she was still sleeping.

Even as roughly spoken as it was, I thrilled when she said my name, which meant she was thinking of me. I realized an interesting truth about myself then: it was imperative that I be important in her life. I had never thought about it before, but as much as I missed Mary, I was also craving being important to Angie.

Feeling restless, I rose and walked through the eerily quiet apartment. Often at night, I heard voices outside. Not tonight. Instead, I heard the persistent slap of the waves, but nothing else. The sound was womblike. I felt as though it was the calm before a storm, and an odd sense of unease began to steal across me. I rubbed my palms over my bare arms for comfort. I was glad I wasn't alone tonight.

After checking the door to the Bookmark to make sure it was firmly locked, I checked the door to the deck outside. Everything seemed secure. I turned off the overhead light in the kitchen, but left on the two lamps in the living room.

Angie remained deeply asleep when I returned to the bedroom. I went quietly through my usual bedtime preparations in the bathroom, and then returned to the bedroom.

I looked down the hall, at the small couch I could easily convert into a cozy bed. I looked at Angie one more time, at her bruises, and carefully joined her under the blankets.

ANGIE

I woke to a horrible pain in my chest and throat and a delightful sensation in my arms. I lay on my side, my arms around Grey, who rested in the front curve of my body. I felt the warmth of Oscar Marie on top of the comforter, tucked into the curve behind my legs. I let my face fall into the sleekness of Grey's flaxen hair. She smelled heavenly. Even though I was in pain and needed to help Mama with breakfast, there was no place on earth I would rather be than right here.

I opened to Grey, but she was still asleep and dreaming. I don't receive dreams well, but I enjoyed the bonding I felt by opening fully with her. I was always afraid to deeply enter the senses of someone I cared about. I didn't want to know too much about how they felt. Mostly because it was an invasion of privacy and secondly, I didn't want some momentary ill will about me to come across. Receiving that kind of information was like being bludgeoned with a weapon. I would not set myself up for that, but here, lying together with Grey sleeping, it felt good to allow the bonding on that intimate, deeper level. I'm not sure I would have done it with her awake, but I had no problem venturing in while she was slumbering. I did feel that her sadness had abated somewhat, which pleased me.

Grey woke slowly, probably disturbed by my slight movements or a change in my breathing patterns. I felt it and began closing off. For a brief moment, she snuggled into my embrace, but realization dawned and I sensed her pulling away.

"Oh, I'm sorry," she murmured, slipping from my arms.

"No." I discovered my throat was raw and the words just wouldn't come out normally. My hands flew to my throat. I managed a whisper. "Not a problem. Like it."

Sitting on her side of the bed, she turned to me. I melted. She looked so beautiful in the early morning sunlight, all warm and tousled from sleep, her hair cascading across her face. Her green eyes were clear and emerald colored this morning.

She saw my neck and sorrow tarnished her gaze. "I am so sorry Mary hurt you."

I wanted to tell her that it may not have been Mary, but didn't feel as though I could get out enough words to explain. She saw my difficulty and rose, showing me a beautiful glimpse of bare thigh below loose tap pants as she shrugged into a long flannel shirt.

"Let me get you something warm to drink," she said. "Coffee. I'll be right back."

After she left the room, Oscar Marie stretched and followed her, so I eased off the bed to my feet. I still wore the shorts and shirt I'd worn yesterday. Stretching my sore body gingerly, I followed them into the kitchen.

Grey was leaning to switch off the lamp in the living room. I became transfixed by her long, tanned legs and the gentle curve of her bottom beneath the silky short pajamas. I felt an uncommon wetness pool in my center, but knew I had to wait until all this haunting craziness was solved before I could acknowledge the depth of my attraction.

"What are you doing out of bed?" she asked while standing in the center of the dining room, her hands on her hips.

I shrugged and splayed my hands helplessly.

She pulled out a chair from the table. "Well, at least sit down. I'll get you some coffee. Do you think you could eat scrambled eggs?"

At my nod, she busied herself in the kitchen. I stared out at the bay and pondered my next move. First, I would pop over and see Mama, and then go home, pack a bag, and come back. I would stay here with Grey until I got to the bottom of this insanity. What did the ghost want from Grey? Obviously, if it *was* Mary, she was violently jealous. I fingered my neck thoughtfully. But what about the attractive redhead? How did she fit into this? I noted the book of poetry. Grey had rescued it from the floor and placed it facedown on the coffee table.

Grey handed me a cup of coffee. I saw its paleness and looked at her quizzically.

"Yes, I added cream. And sugar. It'll soothe your throat. Deal with it." She disappeared back into the kitchen.

I had to chuckle to myself, even though it hurt. One just didn't say no to Grey Graham.

I sipped the coffee and indeed, it was soothing. I drained the cup just as she set before me a plate of softly scrambled eggs with a side of mixed fresh fruit cut into very small pieces. She took my cup and refilled it while I dug in. She joined me moments later and we breakfasted in companionable silence.

"It's good having you here," she said finally. "Comforting. I'm glad I don't have to go through this insanity alone."

Nodding, I found I could speak again, albeit roughly. "You shouldn't. I'll be here until its over."

"You know," she began, idly smoothing her thumb against her ceramic cup. "My mother was a big believer in ghosts. I always thought she was blowing smoke, trying to scare me. I'll never doubt her again."

"Life changing," I agreed.

I thought about Mama's stance on ghosts and realized that it wasn't something we'd ever talked seriously about. I wondered about Grey's relationship with her parents.

"Where are your parents?" I asked.

"Mother died of breast cancer when I was sixteen…"

I grasped her hand across the table, feeling her loss. She looked at our clasped hands, but let them remain together as she continued.

"My father remarried. To a woman he worked with. They moved to Wyoming so I don't see them but once a year."

"Siblings?" I released her hand after seeing her mother's face. Grey looked much like her.

"Nope, an only kid. That's why I started cartooning, I think. To make friends for myself." She smiled. "Suzy is actually my longlost older sister."

I returned her smile. "Me too," I whispered. "Just me and Mama."

"Your mother is sweet," she said, cocking her head and studying me. "I like her a lot."

I nodded, and then laboriously explained my plans for the day.

She glanced around the apartment. "How about I go with you? Would you mind?"

I captured her gaze. Something passed between us, as solid and tangible as the dishes on the table. I realized anew that we would be together. I saw that she was coming to understand it as well. Not on that psychic level where I lived, but on her own earthly plane. I think she knew we'd found one another at last. That she had found her home in me.

"Come with me," I whispered.

Grey blushed, the crimson starting at her smooth neckline and moving upward to her hairline. "I'll…I'll get ready," she said quickly.

GREY

It was good seeing Angie's mother, Maylie, again, but I'm not a hundred percent sure she accepted our abbreviated account of how Angie got hurt. She kept looking at me like I had done it, which perplexed me. I didn't want to give credence to the idea by mentioning it, yet at the same time, I wanted to reassure her I would never deliberately hurt Angie. Never.

We spent a good half hour trying to get Angie the day off, as Maylie made a few calls to find people who could cover her daughter's obviously day-long shift. I realized then how much of a partnership the two women had in operating the business.

I sat at the bar, observing and sipping even more coffee, and watching the weather on the television behind the rail. A storm was brewing. There was much debate about how low in the nation the front would drop.

Dallas would be affected for sure, but the storm was slated to dip as low as Houston. I knew Houston was prone to severe flooding, so hoped the bad weather wouldn't linger long. The forecast called for several inches of driving rain, high winds and lightning.

"Okay," Angie whispered, approaching me from behind and laying a hand on my shoulder. She glanced at the television briefly and shook her head as if in disbelief.

I followed her to her Jeep. We had a pleasant ride through Port Isabel and out into the Fingers region that I had read about in the brochures. We passed a large, formal yacht club and a quiet residential neighborhood, and then we were at a small cottage— Angie's place. The small home fronted North Shore Drive, but the back appeared to open right onto Laguna Madre Bay.

"Wow, you live out here? This is still part of the Fingers area, right?" I asked.

Angie came around the Jeep and took my hand, silently leading me across her front yard and to the far side of the house. From there, I could see, stretching off to my left, the true Fingers with their homes and condos reaching all the way to the water. Most of the homes had extensive decking that reached out into each wide channel. Waterfowl were everywhere, pelicans even roosting outside residential doorways. I noted that just about every home had a boat moored into a type of floating garage or dry dock below the building proper.

The area was like photos I had seen of Venice, Italy with narrow peninsulas of building crowded land stretching out into shallow waterways that were used like highways. It might have been smaller and shallower here perhaps, but I'd never seen the like in real life. I had a sudden urge to kayak between the homes. I laughed at the folly of that idea. I'm sure I would be topsy-turvy and underwater in no time.

I turned to Angie and saw her watching me, her eyes filled with a serene fondness. I leaned into her and kissed her. It happened without warning, without plan. I just felt drawn in and unable to help myself. There was something about Angie, something special.

The kiss was innocent at first, but one of Angie's powerful arms went around my waist. I was crushed into her body and I suddenly wanted more. My mouth opened for her. I invited her to fill me with her essence.

The kiss deepened. The world disappeared, snatched away into the ever-present sea breeze. All I felt was Angie's wind-roughened lips against mine. She smelled like the ocean and earth blended, a powerful aphrodisiac that shot through me, igniting feelings that had been dormant too long. My desire swelled, my body rising like the ocean at high tide.

I pressed against her, my breasts and pelvis soft cushions between us. My hands left Angie's arms and roamed along her upper chest to feel the hard planes of muscle I had sensed there. I cupped her head in my hands even as her hands moved lower on my back, grasping my bottom and pressing me into her even harder.

A hiss of pain doused cold water on our union. I realized I had inadvertently touched the bruises on her neck. I stepped back quickly, moving to the distance of her outstretched arm. Her hand still held mine by the fingertips. Her eyes were dark pools of slate blue desire.

We were both breathing heavily. We studied one another for the better part of a minute as the world returned with boat sounds, people sounds, and the sounds of water and wind.

She smiled at me, an indulgent smile of promise. I know my face and neck had turned bright red. She grasped my hand more tightly and pulled me toward the cottage door. I hesitated.

"I'll behave," she croaked, seeing my doubt. "Promise."

I followed her inside, wondering if *I* could behave.

Her cottage consisted of three large open rooms. I noticed right away that Angie lived very simply. She had only a few pieces of furniture including a sofa, which she pressed me into, an easy chair and a coffee table with only a candle on it. The kitchen was as neat and simple as the main room. She headed there and returned with two bottles of water from the small refrigerator.

"Wait for me. I'm gonna shower and change, okay?" she whispered.

I nodded. One of her hands gently brushed my cheek as she moved away. I keenly felt her absence and mentally shook myself.

Standing, I wandered across the room to the sliding glass doors. The bay stretched before me in its own particular glory. The waves heaved, with froth like white lace slapping against the breakwater below Angie's private deck.

What was I thinking, trusting Angie? Surely this…was she seducing me? I whirled and looked at the interior of the cottage. So many things remained unexplained.

I wanted to take her at face value, but had to wonder what the money was for—a matter of financial need, or was she one of those con artists I'd read about who prey on wealthy tourists? Maybe she was a drug addict.

I strode into the kitchen and guiltily opened a few cupboards. Angie had the bare necessities only: a few dishes, a handful of mismatched silverware. A laptop computer rested on the bar separating the kitchen and living room. I noted a pet bowl and a small bag of cat food, but no cat that I could see.

I strode across the main room and peered into the bedroom. The double bed was made haphazardly, the clothes Angie had been wearing tossed across the foot of it. I saw a tall bureau and a mirror hanging on the partially open bathroom door, but that was all.

I heard the shower running. Steam had already frosted the face of the tall, thin mirror. A huge trusting part of me wanted to go join Angie in the shower. But that other part, the part that told me about my vulnerability since Mary's death, kept me paralyzed.

The noise of the water switched off abruptly. I rushed back to the sofa, my breathing ragged.

ANGIE

We drove back to Grey's house slowly on a meandering, sight-seeing path. I wanted Grey to see Port Isabel from a native's viewpoint. We went out North Shore and came back in along Trout and up Island Avenue so she could get a good feeling about all the Fingers.

I drove along back roads, showing her secret inlets that the tourists knew nothing about. We stopped and watched a congregation of egrets and a tall, dour, great blue heron as he high-stepped among them. We searched for dolphins off Pompano, but didn't have much luck.

It was fun racing along the wind with her, and fun having an entire Saturday off work.

I was still warmed by that incredible kiss we'd shared and I was flying high. She seemed subdued, though. I hoped she wasn't already regretting that moment of bliss.

I figured she was thinking about Mary. I had felt her sadness about Mary's death, so I knew it still affected her, but I was patient. I would wait for her to heal and certainly would not push for anything more in the meantime.

It was late afternoon by the time we got back to Grey's house. We had stopped at Pirate's Landing for shrimp baskets, which we ate sitting out on her deck as the sun made ready for bed.

"Why do you think Mary is doing this to me, Angie?" Grey asked quietly. The ruddy glow of the lowering sun rested on her fine features when she turned her face toward the water.

I lifted an ankle and rested it on my opposite knee, chewing as I gave her question some thought. I took a large gulp of water so I could more easily swallow with my still smarting throat.

"I'm not sure," I finally said. "You say your relationship was a good one. Maybe she *is* angry that you are living on. Doesn't understand it."

"But why attack you, though?"

"Jealousy?" I offered.

She stood and carried her basket into the house. I followed, puzzled by her abruptness. I tossed the remains of my meal in the trash bin and opened my mouth to speak, to ask what was bothering her. She spoke before I could get my words out.

"I need to work. Need to repair that panel. It has to be mailed out on Monday morning." The grimness of her mouth put me off.

I decided to retreat and give her some space. "Sure. I'll spend some time in the Bookmark, see if I can pick up something," I whispered.

"Good idea," she said, turning and perching on the high stool at the drafting table.

I retrieved the poetry book from the coffee table. If there were any answers, I believed they were connected to this book somehow. I needed to open to it to see if I could glean some information.

The Bookmark glowed with a dim ruby sheen from the sunset over the bay. I closed the door to the apartment, but was surprised when Grey snatched the door from my hands.

"Angie. Be careful," she said, her eyes searching my face. "If anything happens, call out or make a noise. I'll hear you, okay?"

I nodded and laid a palm on her shoulder for reassurance. Nothing penetrated to me through the fabric of her T-shirt, but I could see the poorly hidden concern in her gaze. She pushed the door closed, but left it ajar about two inches.

I moved into the room and switched on several lamps before taking a seat in an easy chair in one of the conversation areas.

I have to admit that I had a moment of flashback, remembering the attack of the previous evening. I steeled myself, knowing that running from my fear would be as productive as teats on a boar hog, as my Mama liked to say. Grey could not have a normal life until this issue was dealt with, and as far as I was concerned, the faster life returned to normal, the better.

I reconsidered my earlier thought. When life returned to normal that meant I would have to return home. Not that home was a bad place, but I was certainly enjoying this rarefied time alone with Grey. The thought of it ending tore at me.

My hands moved up to touch my throat. This was a dangerous situation. I needed to resolve it somehow, and quickly, before more havoc hurt one of us more permanently.

Sighing, I placed the book on my knees and scrubbed my palms against my denim shorts. It was time.

I lifted the book and held it flat between my palms. I took a deep breath and opened to it.

GREY

My Anna
You are
abandoned
Forgive my lie

My love lives on
Yet I weep

My world is

Darkened
Without your
Smile

I decided to jot the poem down on my notepad before I blotted it out of my cartoon strip. Just in case we needed it. I read the phrases line by line as I whited them out with correction fluid. I tried to make sense of them. Someone named Anna had been abandoned, but is still loved by someone who misses her. I wondered suddenly if Mary had had another girlfriend when she was alive. Was she looking for her even after death?

"What do you think, Ossie? Would Mama Mary have done that to us?" I looked into the cat's sleepy golden eyes, resting at half-mast, and she twitched her tail at me in answer. "Yeah, I don't think so either but I have to tell you, I'm a little perplexed by this whole poetry thing."

She closed her eyes. I took that as a clear reprimand to get my butt back to work.

I studied the panel. Part of Mister Marks's face was obliterated, as well as his thumb, and the outer corner of Suzy's desk would have to be replaced. Luckily, I hadn't done shading or background work, or I would have had to redo that whole panel, if not the entire strip.

I pulled together my tools as I idly wondered what Angie was doing. I shook my head to clear it. Seemed like every other thought was about Angie now. I was getting a little rankled. The best course of action would be to keep her on task until we discovered what it was Mary wanted. That way she could go back to her bewildering life, and I could get on with the business of healing and getting Mary's Bookmark off the ground.

I suddenly remembered the grand opening and made a mental note to draw the flyers and put them around town in all the local businesses early next week. Spring break was starting. I hoped to generate a little interest among the college crowd who were used to coffeehouses filled with books—probably a useless endeavor as most of them come to South Padre to stay blitzed out of their minds for an entire week. Still, I counted it a good starting point.

I turned my attention back to the strip. I'd never had such a hard time focusing on my work. Even after Mary's death, I had been able to pay attention and get the job done. I chewed my bottom lip. Between Mary's ghost and Angie's distracting presence, I wasn't doing too well.

I pushed the disturbing thoughts away. Using my ruler, I crafted straight lines that would combine to form the usual backdrop for Sassy Suzy's office.

Her office was glassed in, and in the background was a busy secretarial pool full of cubicles and busily moving people. I sketched them in, using well remembered movements to create well remembered characters. Even though the work was repetitious, I still loved cartooning. I liked coming up with clever jokes that fit my characters' personalities. I liked placing props in strategic locations. I liked the artistic processes of crafting space and time to convey an idea to my readers. I'd discovered nothing else in my life to date that quite matched the satisfaction I gleaned from my chosen profession.

I opened my watercolors and took my favorite brush from the slotted jar of water on my worktable. I shaded Suzy's skirt with a subtle wash of color, swiping across each of the five panels for consistency. I tended to stick pretty close to the CMYK color model consisting of cyan, magenta, yellow and black. I usually used a stock cerulean for the blue. I couldn't reproduce magenta, so I would overlap the blue and yellow when needed.

I used blue for the skirt, so I chose yellow for the cardigan. Mister Marks's suit would be my usual blue mixed with some black. I had just finished the last wash of the boss's suit when I felt eyes on me. I smiled and leaned back.

"So what do you think? Looks pretty good. You can't even tell where I had to fix it."

When there was no response at all, I suddenly knew it

wasn't Angie behind me. My breath hitched in my throat and I felt adrenaline flood my system. Thankfully, I had closed the dining room drapes, so there was no reflection in the windows to further torment me. I couldn't turn around, even when the breath coming from my mouth condensed to a white cloud in the frigid, frigid air surrounding me.

"Please," I whimpered. "Please go away. I can't love you like this, Mary. I just can't."

The presence lingered a moment longer, and then thankfully moved away. I heard a volley of unintelligible whispers and a wail before I felt alone again. I slowly turned to the door of the Bookmark and saw jerky movement behind the vertical parting between door and jamb.

I steeled myself and stepped off the stool. I approached the door cautiously, smelling cigarette smoke.

"Angie? Everything okay in there?" My voice sounded the way I felt, choked up and terrified. "I just had kind of a...weird..."

I opened the door and stepped into the Bookmark. The scream ripped from my throat before my mind even registered what I was seeing.

Down at the end of the room, by the double front doors, Angie floated in midair high off the floor. She was on her back, her head and all four limbs drooping as though she was supported by a thick center post. She was spinning slowly. As her head passed by, I saw her eyes were open and unfocused. Her mouth gaped. Her eyes looked milky.

I suddenly realized that this beautiful, vibrant woman was dead.

ELEANOR

"Who is this woman you want me to see?" Robbie asked, walking beside me.

It was as cold as an underground tomb. We were both hunkered down in our woolen peacoats, our breath clouding the path in front of us, our hands stuffed in our pockets. New York City wasn't feeling the cold, however, and the Village was full of pedestrians, as usual.

"I don't know her name," I told him, flicking my cigarette butt into the gutter. "She bartends over at the The Nip. I was reading there last night, and we couldn't take our eyes off one another."

"Did you talk?"

"Nope, she got off shift, I guess, and didn't wait around. Pissed me off, but what could I do?" I stepped off the curb at Fortieth and narrowly missed being cut down by a taxicab whose driver wore thick black glasses. "Get a new pair!" I yelled after him. He flipped me the bird. "So you're reading there tonight too?"

Robbie nodded and freed a hand to scratch at his short beard. "Gonna read 'Qualities of Green.' What are you reading?"

"I'm reading 'Loose Stars,' I think." I felt to make sure my notebook was still tucked under my arm. "Glad we get a meal out of this one." My stomach complained loudly.

"We should, for what they're paying. Are you staying at Edie's tonight?"

I nodded and hitched my collar higher. Thank goodness my short boots were still in good shape, not letting in cold air. I had borrowed a pair of socks from Edie's drawer and I praised that decision all the way down the street.

"I'm going home with Franklin and Emmy." His self-satisfied smile extended all the way to his brown eyes.

I laughed as we approached the door of The Nip. "They still have the hots for you? You must be pushing all the right buttons."

He shrugged and grinned when I opened the door for him.

***

She was there, her thick red hair swept to one side and fastened close to her neck. She wore a black turtleneck and skintight jeans with ballet flats.

I could see behind the bar from my perch atop the barstool the manager had set up for me on the high wooden stage. I had a hard time focusing on the words I needed to read while I watched her flitting around.

The spotlight clicked on me. I lifted my gaze to the people sitting at the dozen or so tables. "This one is called 'Loose Stars.' Questions after." I cleared my throat.

Diamonds fall
From politician
Lips
As lies rise
And become stars
On my horizon

When guns lie
Snuggled
Babies die
Mugged by
Death and
Diamonds

Buy the guns
Feed them
Feed them
inane children
Open lips
Taking in
Stars of Diamonds
and death

I bowed my head. The room erupted into busy conversation. A young girl with dark hair and glasses stood up in the dimness. I'd seen her around Columbia, but hadn't met her.

"Name?" I asked.

"I'm Corrine."

"Yes, Corrine. You have a question?"

She squirmed visibly. "I just love your work," she said. "When *Icebox* came out, I couldn't get to the student bookstore fast enough and they only had two copies left. I bought both."

She paused and took in air, clearly embarrassed by her admission. "My question is about your writing process. Do you prefer to write in coffeehouses, out in nature, or at your home?"

I smiled at her. "Oh, man, thank you for liking my stuff." I was flattered by her obvious adoration and wanted to give her a good answer. "I usually start a dialogue when we're all around the table, you know, like talking, and I get some image, you know, and I just follow it. Doesn't matter where I am. I just follow the muse. Do you write?"

Her eyes grew wide. "Oh, no way, man. Just for school."

I nodded my understanding as a young man stood. I answered about six other questions and was just going to signal the spot guy when another question rang out.

"By children, do you mean actual children, or just the innocence in us that has been lied to for so long?"

Ah, it was the red-headed barkeep and she got it! She watched me expectantly. I grinned at her. "Exactly!"

She smiled seductively and I swear I started to salivate.

Robbie broke my trance. He snapped his fingers repeatedly at me in applause. I moved aside and he took my place on the high stool. He slowly began reading his work. I took comfort from his strong, familiar baritone. I sidled to the bar and lit a cigarette.

The redhead came over and handed me a drink with a lemon twist. "Sidecar, right?"

"Cool. You remembered."

Her gaze smoldered. "Yes, I did." She extended a slim, elegant hand. "I'm Annalise."

"Eleanor." I took the hand, finding it cool and smooth.

"I know," she said.

I blushed.

***

Her skin was like alabaster and just as cool and smooth. I dripped cognac on it just to see if I could warm it with the aged brandy. I licked the cognac off slowly, warming her skin with my heated breath. Propped up on her elbows, Annalise watched me with amusement residing in her dusky blue eyes.

"What are you doing?" she asked.

"Warming you." I moved lower to the ruddy cleft between her legs. I tipped my glass again and rivulets of brandy became lost in the pale, reddish hair there.

"Yes, I'm getting very warm," she gasped, tossing back her head.

I let my tongue lap the cognac from her pubis slowly, lingering at the hidden folds of delight I found there. She slowly relaxed backward and lifted a slender leg to wrap around my shoulders, making sure I stayed close.

"Warm me some more, you incredibly sexy woman."

I did as I was told, losing myself in her soft folds. My hands moved to tease at the marvelously small nipples on pale mounds of flesh. They grew harder, hotter under my fingertips, and she moaned, whispering my name and her need.

Soon there was a tempest of heat and fluid. I felt her rise against my mouth. I lowered an arm and held her there firm as I devoured her passion and made it my own.

Her hands found my hair. She wound her fingers into it, pushing me against her harder and harder until she shuddered into me, my mouth filling with her nectar. I rode her until she stilled then I fell aside, my head resting on her thigh. Her fingers continued to play with my hair as her breathing slowed.

***

"Look what I have for us," Annalise said, drawing me into the room. I nodded at Clark and Stephen, who were crouched over the coffee table sucking leisurely on a hookah. The rich burnt smell of hash filled my nostrils. I had no time to chat since Annalise pulled me past them and into the kitchen. They laughed and waved as I stumbled by.

An oddly shaped wine bottle filled with green liquid stood on the counter. Annalise lifted it and fetched two wineglasses from the cupboard. "This is absinthe," she said in a low, excited voice. "Warren brought it from Germany."

I took a seat at the table and examined the oddity. The ornate, beautiful label was written in German. I couldn't understand much of it.

Annalise returned with a box of sugar cubes and two spoons which she placed on the table.

"I've never had this. What's it like?" I asked.

"I love it. The taste is kinda spicy, minty, but like grass too. You know, like it actually tastes green," she said with a short laugh. "You'll either love it or hate it."

I nodded with enthusiasm. "Cool, man. Let's try it." I watched avidly as she poured several fingers of the crystal green wine in each glass. "I've never seen green wine before."

She shook her head and fished out several sugar cubes from their yellow box. "It's not wine, really, it's like whisky and will get you so loaded."

"So it's strong."

She nodded as she placed two sugar cubes in a spoon and then carefully poured hot water from a pan on the stove over them. They dissolved and soon I had my first sip of absinthe. The sugar syrup rested on the surface like a sheen of sweet sweat, glazing my upper lip as the potent liquor warmed my throat and chest. The taste was like licorice, but made more pungent by the high alcohol content. After the first glass, I was feeling no pain and was also emboldened enough to speak my mind.

"Annalise?"

"Yeah, baby?" Our hands were entwined on the wooden tabletop as we enjoyed the mellow glow of the green fairy, as she had called it.

"You know we've been together almost nine months now…"

She smiled dreamily at me. "A perfect nine months," she added.

I smiled back at her. "Yes, a perfect nine months. And I'm thinking that maybe we could give that western trip a try. What do you think?"

"You mean the exodus to Berkeley?"

"Yes, a change might be nice."

"But my job." She sat back, her eyes searching my face.

"Well, I…I won't go without you. That's what I wanted to tell you."

She looked at me and smiled her sexy, inviting smile. "But you want to go, don't you?"

I looked away, feeling sheepish. "Well, I am tired of freezing every winter, and *Abandoned* is out and is done making the rounds here in the city. We could take it west."

"True," she agreed. "And I'm tired of the cold too. You know, I could barkeep anywhere, and I could certainly start a new semester out there."

I studied her, hoping I'd heard her right. "You mean…?"

She nodded sharply. "Let's do it! With you by my side, it'll be wonderful."

***

Images of palm trees filled my mind, and of Annalise in one of those new bikini bathing suits. I smiled at my lechery and knew it had been enhanced by the absinthe. As if I hadn't had enough of her gorgeous body and her absinthe from early evening until four in the morning.

I glanced at the dim dawning light. Fall was starting and my feet crunched a few early leaf deserters as I made my way up the lawn to cross onto Forty-Second.

The packing had been fun, trying to decide which token coat Annalise would take with her. We finally decided on a cool, lightweight trench coat with a liner that could be easily removed. And then I removed the entire coat and made love to my Anna, again and again.

Poems about it roiled in my mind. I couldn't wait to get home to my notebook and jot them down. I also needed to pack up a few last things from Edie's house. It was probably a good idea for me to move on anyway. Her place was getting crowded.

A sudden noise descended on me. I turned just as two huge Checker cabs came racing each other around the corner of Forty-Second and Fifth.

I was too far into the street. I panicked and moved to run across just as one cab swerved to miss me. My last thought was about Annalise and whether she would think I had gone west without her.

GREY

Anger and grief warred within me as I rushed across the room and reached up a tentative hand to take one of Angie's freezing cold hands in mine. How could Mary be so cruel? I hated her in that instant.

When my hand met Angie's, a strange stillness filled the room. A warm breeze rushed past me and Angie dropped from her pivotal point in the air. I tried to catch her when she fell, but her deadweight caused us both to plummet to the carpet.

I rested under her supine body, my heart breaking. Tears cascaded down my face and huge sobs tore from me. I cried for what seemed like an eternity until the warmth of Angie's body—and the subtle movement of her chest—penetrated my grief.

Quickly, I scurried out from beneath her until I could see her face with its closed eyes and normal color. She breathed! Pleasure filled me so fully that I found it hard to speak. Instead, I just pressed my cheek to hers and sobbed anew, but this time from happiness.

I felt her arms come up and weakly enfold me. A hand gently caressed my back. I leaned into her, suddenly and unexpectedly crying out all my grief from Mary's untimely death. Tears rolled from me in an unceasing river, spreading to dampen the shoulder of Angie's shirt. Harsh sobs shook my body. Even though I was embarrassed to break down in front of her, there was nothing I could do. I cried until I could cry no more.

Angie murmured soft phrases of comfort in my ear, but allowed me to weep on unabated. When I finally stilled, hiccupping and trying to breath, she stirred.

I mopped my face on the sleeve of my T-shirt and moved to help ease her into a nearby chair. "Oh, my God, Angie. What happened to you?"

She peered at me in confusion. "What?" she croaked.

"We need to get you some water," I told her. "Can you walk into the apartment?"

I helped her to her feet, then held her upright as she swayed alarmingly. We walked together slowly.

"How could you do that?" I asked. "I mean, I've never…" I quieted when we entered the apartment. I sat her at the table and placed a cool bottle of water in front of her. I took a seat opposite her while she drank.

"Do you always do that?" I asked, studying her. "I really thought you were dead. Even your eyes were like all white… not like rolled back in your head, but like cloudy, milky. It was so creepy. How do you do that?"

Angie watched me for a long beat, and then that all-American smile flashed at me. I relaxed, tension fading away that I didn't even know had built up again.

"I have no idea what you are talking about, hon," she said.

I was perplexed. "So it's like a trance. But I mean...you were floating in the air!"

She eyed me doubtfully. "Floating? I don't think so."

"But I saw you, Ange. You were a good four or five feet up in the air. On your back. I swear it."

"Seriously? I've never...never had anything like that happen before."

"Did you see anything in the trance? What did you see? Did you see Mary?" I leapt to my feet and fetched her a picture from the wallet in my handbag. "This is her. Were you able to ask her why—"

Angie took the picture with one hand. The other pressed a quieting finger to my lips.

"Slow," she whispered. "Slow, please. My head feels really funny and you just need to slow down a little, sweetheart."

I had no control over the way my heart swelled when she said the endearment, but I tried to ignore it. "Sorry. This is Mary. Was she there? Did you talk to her?" She looked at the photo, but I could tell she was having a hard time seeing it. Guilt filled me. "Oh, Angie, put that down. You need to rest."

I grabbed the duffel bag she'd left near the sofa and forced her to follow me down the hall. I pushed her into the bathroom and handed her the duffel. "Do you need me to help you dress for bed?"

She looked at me and gave me one of her damned seductive smiles. "Oh, I'd be happy for the help."

"I'll be out here if you need me." I smirked at her and shut the door.

ANGIE

I studied the photo Grey pressed upon me, stalling for time. I knew now that this haunting had nothing to do with Mary. I didn't remember specifics, but I knew the ghost was Eleanor Copeland. I wasn't sure what she wanted, but I hoped telling me her story had been enough, and now she would move on and leave Grey alone.

I looked down at the photo of the pleasant-looking butch woman Grey had loved, and realized that I didn't want all this to be over. As soon as I told Grey the truth, that it wasn't Mary, and that nothing was needed from Grey for her dead lover to be at rest, this intimate time with her would come to an end. I didn't want it to end.

As she drew me down the hallway to her bedroom, I had a momentary fantasy that she brought me there willingly, to lie with her and share a night of profound pleasure that would cement us as a couple. In my mind, she wanted me as much as I wanted her.

Then I was in the bathroom alone, my duffel bag at my feet. I sighed and got ready for bed, nervous about where I would be sleeping tonight.

I shook my head and splashed cold water on my face, trying to clear my mind. I nudged my memory, trying to recapture the time I'd spent in trance. I retained some impressions and could still taste Eleanor's cigarettes.

I knew the time period Eleanor had lived in was the mid-forties and early fifties, and that she was heavily involved in the culture of the Beat era. And she lived in New York City.

I remembered how Eleanor had loved Annalise, but this vision was very different than ones I had dealt with before. Always in the past, the spirit had actually approached me and sent the visions to me. This one had sucked me in so that I lived it *as* Eleanor.

I still had no clue what she wanted from Grey and that really bothered me. I didn't like being confused, once again dealing with things so far removed from my control.

I sighed and stepped from the bathroom. The bedroom was deserted.

When I went looking for Grey, I found her at her drawing table, sipping wine and looking at the Sassy Suzy strip.

"Everything okay?" I whispered cautiously. The strip looked great, like it was all finished.

She looked up. "So far. The wine's on the counter if you want some."

"Thanks." I saw that she had left a glass out for me, so I

poured a healthy serving and took a deep draught. "What a crazy couple of days, huh?"

She nodded and lifted her eyes, which looked hollowed and drawn dark by fear. "I'm exhausted. Do you think she will do anything else tonight?"

I shrugged and noticed a blanket and pillow on the sofa. I felt crushed.

"How are you feeling?" she asked, searching my face.

"I'll be fine. I just need to piece together what I saw so I can explain it, okay?"

"Sure. I'm not trying to pressure you. I just want it to be over."

"I know you do. Listen," I indicated the comic strip. "Have you got anywhere safe you can put that?"

"As if," she muttered. "I think Mary could damage it no matter what, if she really wanted to. She knows how important this strip is to me. I don't appreciate her taking her anger out on it."

Yet she lifted the strip and placed it inside a huge portfolio that she pulled out from under the drafting table. She switched off the small light on the table. We stood silently for a handful of heartbeats.

"Well, I guess we'd better try and get some sleep," I said. "I promised Mama I'd come in tomorrow. Spring break is starting up and things are getting busy."

"I didn't realize you managed the restaurant with your mother. Sorry about that."

"That's okay." There was so much I wanted to say to her. I felt hampered, though, and could only watch her.

Grey turned away. "Let me know if you need anything, okay? I'll be right out here."

She moved to the sofa and started making up a bed. A powerful sureness grew in me and I moved to still her hands. I made her look at me and wordlessly shook my head. I pulled her gently along the hall to the bedroom, our gazes interlocked. I sensed her fear and made sure I was as gentle and loving in my actions as I could be.

In the bedroom, I nudged her toward the bathroom. "Go change. I just want to hold you, Grey. That's all."

Relief flooded her features. I recaptured her hand to see if my advances were unwelcome. All I saw was that she was afraid and didn't want to be alone. I released her hand. That was enough for me.

GREY

I awoke the next morning in Angie's arms and realized how well rested I felt. I'd slept like a baby all night. The fact that she hadn't tried to seduce me leapt into my mind as soon as I awakened. Lying there, I pondered the issue a good while. Was it because she didn't want me? Or did she actually want to protect me and make me feel safe?

"What time is it?" she asked. One of her arms still rested on my waist. She tightened it, pulling me secure.

"About eight," I replied, glancing at the clock. "Hey, your voice is better."

She chuckled. "About time. How did you sleep?"

"Amazingly well. Guess it helps to have my protector close."

"Some protector I am. I got myself strangled and floated around the reading room. That's helpful." She laughed ruefully.

"It still felt good to have you here," I admitted.

"So." She sighed. I felt her chest swell behind my back. "Since we're not distracted by looking at one another, wanna tell me how you feel…about us?"

"What do you mean?" I touched her hand where it pressed against my stomach. I needed to escape, but loved the feel of her against me.

"You sense it as much as I do. That we're supposed to be together." Her voice was quiet and thoughtful.

"How can you know something like that? I can't know that."

Silence grew between us. I had to admit to myself I did feel the energy connecting us, just as surely as I'd felt Mary's energy yesterday. Guilt filled me. Mary. How could I think of loving another?

"You'll never stop loving her," Angie said in a low voice. "You need to accept that and move on. Your heart is big enough to love us both."

Tears welled in my eyes. I realized suddenly that I *did* love them both. And as much as I felt the cavernous emptiness from Mary's removal from my life, I knew if I lost Angie, it would be just as painful. As if she sensed my distress, Angie buried her face in my hair and held me close. I had no response, or at least not one that I felt I needed to put into words.

We stayed that way a good while, silently drinking in one another. Angie finally sighed and moved onto her back. "Well, as nice as this is, I guess it's just about time to go to work. Want to have brekky with me at Mama's?"

I turned over and peeped at her from behind my pillow. I felt renewed, playful even. "I do. Can she do pancakes?"

"Can she do pancakes? Honey, you are talking about the pancake queen! They are so light and airy, you'd think she mixed them from clouds."

I cocked an eyebrow at her and lifted up on one elbow. "You sound like a commercial."

She laughed and rolled to her feet. She stretched and touched her toes ten times. "Can I use the shower?"

I stretched out flat in the bed, surrounded by quilts still warm from her body. "Of course. Just save me some hot water."

As soon as I heard the water start, I had to run into the Bookmark and use the public restroom. Restless Mary had been at it again. The paper towel holder, which fed towels by a motion sensor, had been practically emptied during the night. I sighed and spoke to her.

"Is it okay, Mary? Is it okay if I love another? Love Angie?"

I felt a sense of warmness steal across me and I felt joy. The first real joy I'd felt since Mary had been taken from me.

In the bedroom, I put a knee on the bed, ready to crawl back into the warmth until Angie was done. Instead, without thinking too much about it, I tapped gently at the door and went in. I stood outside the glass door of the shower for a long beat as Angie watched me from the other side. She moved the door open about six inches and held out a hand to me in invitation.

I stepped out of my pajamas and stepped fearlessly into her arms.

She lifted my chin and pressed her wet lips to mine. The scents of soap and shampoo surrounded me as her kiss conquered me. My legs grew weak under the gentle onslaught. I felt my center liquefy and craved her with almost painful demand.

Her strong hands found my waist and caressed me there. I lifted my arms and cradled her head as our kiss transported me. Much later, her hands moved up my waist to cup my breasts, her fingertips moving sensually against my nipples, sending rockets of pure sensation through me.

I spread Angie's legs with my knee and pressed my vulva against her thigh, hoping she could feel the swelling her touch caused.

She moaned into my mouth. I felt her hot breathing increase. I depressed the pump for the liquid soap and soaped our bellies and backs. The soap glided like quicksilver, leaving trails of slippery flesh and suds. She copied me and soaped my breasts, looking into my eyes as she teased the area from breast to neck.

Her gaze was hard with desire. She moved her hands under my arms, the pressure just shy of tickling, and used those hands to lift me to her lips again. I whimpered at the possession.

After kissing me thoroughly, she lowered a hand and touched me there, where I wanted her the most. I arched into her, the autonomic response beyond my control. The soap and my arousal allowed her to slip easily inside. She moaned and fell against me. I was cradled into the curve of her body and her arm against the wall of the shower as she pushed into me, riding my thigh while she pushed rhythmically against my clit and the slick area behind it.

Our lips found each other and meshed. Passion became a physical thing that occupied the shower with us. My mouth fell open as every move of her body pressed against my newly sensitive breasts, making my body clench against her fingers again and again until I felt the overwhelming rush of orgasm swell and break like storm-tossed waves against Angie's hand.

She slowly stilled her hand, but leaned in to suckle my breasts, extending the orgasm and wringing gasps of satiation from me. Thank goodness she was strong enough to hold me upright because I was limp from the power of that shuddering release.

Slowly, she soaped my body again and shampooed my hair, her fingers mesmerizing in their powerful adeptness. I hugged her close when she rinsed my hair and body, wanting to convey closeness and love. She turned off the cooling water and continued to hold me, pressing gentle kisses to the top of my head.

ANGIE

Mary came to me on Sunday about midday. I must have been distracted or have let my guard down while pondering the Eleanor issue so intensely. One minute I was alone in the kitchen double-checking a to-go order, and there she was standing on the other side of the dough board. She was dressed simply in jeans and a dark green T-shirt, but it was Mary.

She looked at me with soulful brown eyes. I felt sadness radiating from her. As usually happens, I was suddenly awash in images. Mary purchasing Eleanor's book in a small bookstore in

Virginia. Mary in a small room crammed floor to ceiling with books, sitting at a desk when Eleanor's book falls open in front of her. Eleanor appeared to Mary. Time passed like the fast forwarding of a videotape. Mary using a laptop and looking for someone...for Annalise.

"You were helping her," I said.

"Helping who?" Mama said behind me. "Do you have Caroline's order?"

I absently handed her the bags. She carried them into the restaurant, leaving me alone with my thoughts. Mary had known what Eleanor needed to move on. It had to do with finding Annalise.

I suddenly knew that was what we had to do, find Annalise and tell her that Eleanor what? Loved her? Well, I would cross that bridge later. For now, I had a clear direction: find Annalise. I smiled and sighed deeply. At last. I silently thanked Mary, promising to care always for Grey, and went back to work.

It took me a good thirty minutes of mentally planning computer searches and waiting on two tables before I realized that Annalise had to be dead as well. Duh. If she had lived her youth in the forties, then her time here on this plane had passed. Depression swamped me. If Annalise was dead as well, why couldn't she and Eleanor find one another? My head reeled.

"You look kinda sick," Gail said, passing by me lugging a bin full of dishes cleared from the tables. "Are you okay?"

"Here, let me help you with that," I said, hurrying to take the heavy bin from her. "Where's Pedro?"

"He ran to the bathroom. I thought I'd bring it in for him."

I looked at Gail's round sweating face and frowned at her. "That's too heavy for you. Next time you come get me or leave it for him."

She grinned at me. "Yes, ma'am!"

I took the bin into the kitchen and started unloading it into the dishwasher.

Pedro rushed in a few minutes later. "No, miss, Pedro will do that." He jumped in.

I went back to take care of my tables.

The storm was the huge topic of conversation. That and my paling purple neck. I just sidestepped most of their questions about the bruises and ignored Sanchez's scriptwriting, contemplating gaze. The storm could not be ignored, however, and an alert had already been issued for the island. I knew that meant The Point would be next.

Mama stood to one side, talking to locals seated at a table. I sidled closer to overhear.

"S'posed to be a bad one," Charlie Reiner said, pointing with a slice of toast to emphasize his words.

"That's what I hear," Mama agreed. "I guess we'll have to close up for the duration. When are they saying it'll hit?"

"Tomorrow night, middle. I guess this'll nix any breakers coming." This was delivered with a petulant pout by Jimmy Chambers, who ran one of the liquor stores on the island. "Like we need more grief after last year's blow."

"Now, Jimmy, you just calm down. You know they're coming. Every hotel on the island is booked to capacity. They won't back out of it just because of this short squall." Mama said, moving aside so Gail could get in and freshen the coffee cups.

"Let's hope it's a short one," said Missy Centavo, owner of Gilda's Boutique. "I still haven't repaired all the wind damage from last year."

Estella Garcia glanced wistfully out the side window. "I guess I'll have a backlog of flowers if they close the causeway. Are they gonna close it, Maylie? Have you heard?"

"Tomorrow night at eight," I offered. "Tunny and the other boys were in talking about it earlier. It'll be on the local news in the morning, they said."

A collective sigh sounded. Dealing with storms rolling through periodically was the price we paid for living in paradise.

I moved away to clear off table sixteen. It was off to itself, and I took a few private moments to think about Grey. She had surprised me deliciously that morning, joining me in the shower.

When I opened to it, even now, I reeled from the passion she carried inside her slender body. I knew already that my need for her in the physical sense was going to be as insatiable as the craving I carried for the rest of her.

I glanced over at table twelve where we'd breakfasted. I could still see her there, her eyes shining as she flirted with me, teasing me for not allowing her to please me the way I'd pleased her. I tucked my head, knowing I was blushing. I eagerly looked forward to tonight when we would take our time and explore one another at length.

GREY

I had witnessed firsthand a phenomenon I had only heard about from newspaper stories. Whenever there was a storm brewing, everyone and his brother went shopping.

I blew sweaty hair off my forehead and carefully backed my SUV into the alley next to my building. All I'd needed was a few groceries and a few things for the Bookmark. Who knew twenty-five people would want generators and plywood at the same time I wanted wooden blinds for the windows?

Grumbling under my breath, I unlocked the side door and

methodically unloaded my purchases from the SUV. I stacked the larger supplies for the Bookmark in the smaller side room and carried a few of the more portable things in to the coffee areas. I locked the SUV. Toting two bags of groceries, I made my way into the apartment.

"Hey, Ossie, Mama's home," I called out as I entered the apartment.

I stopped. Both cloth bags dropped from my hands and landed on the carpeted floor. Oranges rolled out and made a slow path directly across the center of the floor where Oscar Marie lay flat on her back, purring as though she were being rubbed. I could actually see the fur on her neck moving as if brushed by an invisible hand. To make matters worse, she lay in a scattered pile of photos that someone had dumped from the photo boxes I had stacked under the television table.

"No, please, don't hurt my cat," I whispered. "Anything but that."

A loud but unintelligible whisper sounded in the room. Oscar Marie leapt to her feet and arched her back. The sound of her loud hiss of anger tore through me.

While I watched her for clues, a dark shadow materialized next to me. I felt an uncommon warmth pass over me as the darkness moved across me and away. I leaned over to pick up Oscar Marie. I cradled her close even though her tail was twitching a dire warning of *don't mess with me*.

I wasn't sure whether I comforted her or she comforted me. I looked down at the photos and saw they were family photos of Mary and me at various functions. I saw several Christmases and Thanksgivings, as well as most of the vacations we had taken during the past ten years.

I walked slowly around the pile, rubbing Oscar Marie and trying to make sense of any message that had been left for me. After a few moments, I placed Oscar Marie on the back of the sofa and pulled out my cell phone. I found and pushed the number Angie had pecked in that morning as I lifted one of the grocery bags and carried it to the kitchen.

"Hey, glad you called," she said. The sound of her voice warmed me in delicious ways. "I was just thinking about you."

"Good thoughts, I hope," I said, eyeing the living room cautiously while I fetched the second bag and gathered the scattered oranges.

"You know it. Is everything okay?"

"I guess." I paused, hating to be forced to deal with this again. "I just wanted to let you know that Mary was here after I got home. She was petting Oscar Marie." I didn't want to mention the photos. It seemed too painful.

"So you saw her?" I could hear dishes clashing in the background.

"Well, it was a shadow, kind of. She didn't hurt me or Ossie, so maybe she's calmed down now," I said hopefully.

"How did Oscar Mayer react?"

I laughed at Angie's pet name for Oscar Marie. "She seemed to be liking it until I scared the spirit off. I think she's a little ticked at me now."

"Well, that shoots down my theory of hoping the ghost had gone away," she said with a deep sigh.

"I guess," I agreed.

"Hey, did you hear about the storm?"

"I did and I've been experiencing the panic firsthand. I'm just now getting home from my trip into town. People were everywhere today."

"Yeah, we've even been swamped here. Things are under control now, though, and I need to go batten down some hatches. Do you wanna go?"

I glanced around the apartment, knowing I'd be stuck there for the next day or so weathering the storm. "Sure. Can I bring Ossie? I have a carrier."

"Sure. You guys come on over when you're ready, and I'll wrap up here."

We signed off. I realized how comforted I'd become just hearing her voice, and wondered if I would always react that way.

I put the groceries away, gathered the photos, and placed them back into their box. I laid my hand on the top of the box for a long moment, knowing that part of my life was definitely over and a new chapter had begun. Now if Mary would realize it, we could all move on.

I sighed and stored the box under the television. I looked at Oscar Marie, standing on the dining table, and asked, "Hey, Ossie, wanna go for a ride in a Jeep?"

ANGIE

Grey was starting to relax.

I sensed a real shift in her mood when she and Oscar Marie met me outside The Fat Mother. I pulled Grey close and planted a kiss on her, letting her know I had *really* missed her, right there on the sidewalk in front of the restaurant. She blushed adorably. With an arm wrapped around me, she led me to the Jeep.

The wind was already up. I turned my eyes west, searching for storm signs. Nothing yet, but I knew from a lifetime lived here that squalls could come on fast enough to take your breath away. I took the carrier from Grey's hands and helped her into the Jeep.

"Hey there, hot dog, ready to go for a ride?" I reached through the metal grate and scratched Oscar Marie's ears. She purred, but still looked around nervously as I buckled her and Grey in securely.

"So where are we going?" Grey asked as I backed the Jeep out of the parking space.

"Well, since we're still ghost hunting, I thought I'd stay with you guys during the storm. If that's okay?" At her nod, I continued. "I need to go drop the shutters on my house and also go batten down the SPICEY."

"The SPICEY. You never did tell me what that is." She donned a large pair of sunglasses and was, if possible, even more adorable than before.

"Ah, that's right, we got sidetracked. It's the South Padre Island Center for Extraordinary Youth. I teach there." I paused when harsh reality washed over me. "Or at least I did."

I pulled up in front of the center and unbuckled Oscar Marie and Grey. I carried the cat carrier and unlocked the door, ushering Grey inside.

"I'm going to make some calls this evening to cancel school tomorrow and the next day, I think. Just to be on the safe side," I told her as we went inside. I switched on the lights. Grey walked into the common area. I set down Oscar Marie's carrier and moved to give Grey a tour.

"This is where we do the lessons," I explained, pointing out the colorful area that held ten desks. We had laid soft, oversized foam tiles on the floor, and their primary colors had been carried up onto the wall with poster board squares. We had a chalkboard that had been donated and the colorful squares outlined it as well. We had tacked up a number of the kids' drawings. I took Grey over and pointed some out to her.

"This is amazing," she said, looking around. "And what do you do over here?"

We moved to the long tables that we used for art projects and for eating our lunches. I explained their use. She touched several castles that had been left there.

"Wow, would you look at these," she exclaimed.

"Yeah," I agreed. "Pretty awesome, huh?"

"And this?" She pointed at Fred's hospital bed.

"We have one little guy. Well, he's a teen, actually, that has pretty severe CP—cerebral palsy. We keep him close so he can participate. He just loves it. We had another bed-bound guy named David, but he passed on a while back. We've actually lost two of our students, but we have a good bunch now. I know one thing, I will sure miss seeing them every day if we have to close for good."

Grey studied my face. "But what has changed?"

"Progress. That's a constant, though, not a change. We have to move out of this building by the first."

"Oh, no, and this is such a good location, close to your other job. Have you found another place yet?"

I took a deep breath. "Not yet. I have some people looking, but most of the places big enough aren't affordable."

Grey grew quiet long enough that it drew my attention. "That's why, isn't it?"

"Why...oh."

"Why I'm paying two thousand dollars. Now I understand."

"I know, honey, and I so apologize for that. I realized as soon as you left how dead wrong that was. That's why I came by that night, to apologize and take it back. To tell you that of course I would help you for nothing. I never got to it because of the cabinets and everything, but that was my intention."

Grey laughed and hung her head, shaking it. "If you only knew what I have been thinking about you," she said teasingly.

I had to share her merriment. "That bad, huh? I can see why you would think some pretty awful stuff about me. I really am sorry, Grey." I leaned and hugged her, my chin on her head.

"Well, I'm sorry that you have to move the kids. Why do you have to leave?"

I told her the story of the grand new marina while I moved around the interior of the building and rolled down the hurricane blinds. Grey helped me lug out our two waterproof plastic tubs. We placed all the records in one and the artwork and books in another. I flipped the seals tight and stacked the tubs in my office. I double-checked the lock on my waterproof moneybox and placed it next to the others.

I locked the office door and took one more quick scan of the classrooms. Everything looked secure. Taking Grey's hand, I picked up Oscar Marie and deposited them both in the Jeep. I walked around the school's exterior, fastening the clasps on the blinds and making sure there were no outside items that would fly away in a strong wind.

"It looks like you've had a lot of practice doing this," Grey said when we pulled out.

I made a face at Oscar Marie, who was peeking at me from inside the carrier. "I grew up here. It's second nature."

"I thought we didn't have as many bad storms here."

"Well, the thing about the storms here is that they're not nearly as powerful as the ones on the east coast, first of all, and in the second place they move through really quickly. This is just going to be a powerful, low pressure system. When it meets the heat of the Gulf waters, it can cause some grief. I don't expect it to be bad." I took her hand to reassure her. "Are you worried?"

She smiled at me and squeezed my hand. "No, not if you are with me. If it was a major hurricane, I might be quaking in my shoes, though."

"Well, we'll get my cottage shored up, and then head back to your place. Who knows? Maybe we can think of something to take your mind off that possibility."

She looked at me and raised an eyebrow. "If we're alone, that is."

I grimaced comically. "Yes, there is that."

GREY

"There's something I need to tell you," Angie said quietly.

I had fixed simple teriyaki noodle bowls for dinner while Angie made her phone calls, and now we were seated out on the dock enjoying the meal and the storm tinged evening. A brisk wind had come up. I could definitely tell the weather was changing.

I took a deep breath. "Is it bad? You're already in a relationship, right?"

She scowled at me. "What? No, silly! I just didn't want to tell you this earlier because…well, because I didn't want you to send me away. I mean, not that I did anything wrong, it's just..." Her voice trailed off.

I waited impatiently.

"The ghost isn't Mary," Angie said finally.

I chewed that morsel of information for a moment or two. "So how do you know this? You did see something, didn't you?"

"Yes." She lifted her bowl and drank the remaining broth, then set the bowl aside. "It's the woman on the book. The author. Her name is Eleanor Copeland, and she was a pretty famous poet back in the forties."

"In New York, right? I read that on the back of the book."

"That's right. Well, Eleanor fell in love with this woman named Annalise, and they were going to go to California together sometime in the early fifties. Unfortunately, Eleanor was hit by a speeding cab before they could leave the city."

Sadness filled me. "That's awful. That must be the Annalise she mentions in those poems."

Angie nodded. "And I think I know what Eleanor wants. Why she's haunting you."

"Well, don't keep me in suspense." I placed my bowl on the rough planking of the floor and waited, clasping my hands together in front of me.

"She wants us to find Annalise."

I watched her, wondering if I'd heard her correctly. "But if they lived back then, Annalise would have to be, like, eighty or ninety years old. She might even be dead herself."

"I know. I thought of that today." Angie sighed.

"Eleanor told you this during that trance you were in?" I tried to wrap my head around this new information.

Angie shook her head slowly. "Well, here's where it gets a little sticky." She paused and moved her hands across her face, scrubbing at it. She eyed me from behind her fingers. "Mary came to me at work today."

I studied her. "No, wait. Why would Mary—" I leapt to my feet, unable to understand and direct my thoughts.

Angie rushed to hold my arms, her expression grim. "Mary came to me, like one of my normal visions. I saw when and where she bought Eleanor's book. Eleanor came to her, haunted her. But Mary figured it out and she was helping Eleanor find Annalise."

"Mary never mentioned this to me. How could she be working on something like that and me not know anything about it? That's just wrong." I studied her face. Could Angie be lying to me? Why would she?

"But honey, Mary showed it to me. I saw her on her computer looking up information about Annalise."

I looked into her eyes and saw the pain there, and the fear that I wouldn't believe her. I realized suddenly that she must face this situation almost every day of her life in one way or another. I had to have faith in her. I had to believe her because I loved her.

I calmed myself. "Did Mary find Annalise?"

Angie released my arms and moved to the railing to peer into the shallows below. "That I don't know. But I believe that's what we need to do to put Eleanor's angry spirit to rest. We need to find Annalise."

I moved to stand at the railing next to her.

"Look," she whispered urgently. I followed her pointing finger and there, glistening in the glow emanating from the condos on the breakwater, was a pod of four dolphins frolicking in the shallows of the bay. We watched them for a long time, the wind whipping fiercely around us, until the dolphins moved too far away for us to see them.

Angie turned to press me against the railing with the length of her body. She stared into my eyes while I wrapped my arms around her muscular waist. "The wind's really getting up," she said calmly.

I returned her penetrating gaze. I wanted this woman so fiercely, I couldn't even think about it in any sort of coherent fashion. She set my blood on fire.

"Kiss me, Angie," I whispered. "I want you so badly."

She closed those magnificent eyes and a low whimper

sounded. Then her lips were on mine and I felt her need as it seared through me. I adored—no, craved—the firm pressure of her strong hands against my back. I loved the long, lean lines of her body when she pressed against me. She fit me perfectly. I felt as though I could never get enough of her touching me, skin to skin, face to face.

Wanting her skin, I broke the kiss and slowly unbuttoned the Oxford shirt she wore above her shorts. I dropped the collar back, exposing her broad, sleek shoulders. She wore a sports bra under the shirt. I slipped my hands underneath so I could caress her breasts and her hardening nipples. I also touched the tight expanse of her belly.

"You feel so good," I whispered, pressing my lips against her ear.

"You *make* me feel so good," she countered, her words falling against my ear like diamonds sliding slowly onto black velvet. She pulled my hands from her skin and drew me into the apartment. She locked the door.

Our clothing fell from us. By the time we reached the bedroom, there were no further barriers to our lovemaking. Angie pressed into me, moving my legs apart, claiming me fully. I lifted my body, pressing into her as much as possible. Our kisses made us one. I wasn't sure if there was any separation anymore.

I turned her onto her back and moved her hands above her head, holding them flat as I kissed along her neck and breasts. I kissed her lips. She lifted her head up eagerly to meet me.

Our tongues played games as our kisses deepened into soul-searing possessions.

I pulled back and straddled her, pressing my hot wetness against her lower belly. Freeing her arms, I cupped my own breasts as I moved against her, slowly pleasuring myself, gasping with erotic joy. She watched me, her hands on my hips, her eyes dark and grim with passion, until she could take no more. She slid her hand between us and entered me hard and deep.

I gasped at this new possession, even as a shudder of release swept over my body. I rode her arm, wrapping my arms around my own shoulders and securing myself when I felt dizziness overtake me.

Then I was on my back. Her mouth was over me, devouring me in that wet center I offered her so readily. Her hands were on my breasts as her tongue brutalized my swollen, sensitive nub, bringing me to the edge of release, then moving to enter me and approach my pleasure from another angle. She did this again and again until I sobbed for release, my body quaking with frantic need.

Apparently sensing this need, she stopped, paused her assault, and dropped her head to my thigh for a brief moment, as if experiencing the sensations fully along with me. When she resumed, her mouth was more gentle and brought me lovingly to that abyss of pleasure and tipped me over. I soared into space, my body rushing headlong until I landed in her arms, her lips pressed to my forehead while she held me close.

ANGIE

I rested next to Grey, my body blazing, experiencing vicariously her passionate release. Her sensual energy amazed me. I reveled in the fire energy between us.

We dozed a long time, but when Grey stirred, she entwined our legs. Her thigh found my wetness. She knew I still craved release, craved her. She tipped me toward her and suckled my breasts as she smiled up into my eyes, hers full of sensual promise.

Earthquakes shifted tectonic plates that had long lain dormant within me. Sound erupted from my lips as Grey alternately suckled and teased the tips of my breasts. One of her hands moved lower to stroke my outer lips, teasing the very end of my clit where it protruded with demanding need.

Grey kissed along my flank, her head under my arm, her hand gently moving against my clit. Her fingers went inside, seeking wetness. When she touched me once more, those tectonic plates moved yet again and a volcano erupted. My breath expelled harshly and my body shook with major tremors. Her fingers pressed in deeply. She pulled upward against the back of my clit until I throbbed helplessly against her hand, my breath rasping against her neck.

Moments later, I opened my eyes and rolled onto my back, and there she was. Eleanor. Standing next to the bed behind Grey, looking at me with milk-white eyes, her long black hair streaming on either side of her thin, pale face.

Shocked beyond belief, I shouted hoarsely, the sound ripped from me involuntarily as I scrambled back toward the headboard, away from the vision.

Grey sat up, alarmed. She saw where my wide eyes focused. Fear etched a furrow in her brow as she studied me. Her breathing became labored.

"What is it?" she whimpered.

I couldn't speak due to my racing heart, but I worked to calm my body, a hand pressed to my thumping chest. Grey turned slowly around as Eleanor, like a projected film gone bad, stuttered into oblivion.

"It was Eleanor," I gasped finally.

"No," Grey moaned, shaking her head and gripping the coverlet against her nakedness. "No."

"That's it! I've had enough," I said, rising and collecting my clothing. "This will stop. One way or another."

GREY

"I don't have Mary's computer, honey. I gave it to her sister because I already had a computer, and she gave it to her daughter to use for school," I said.

Angie paced the kitchen, both hands cradling the warmth of her ceramic mug of hot tea. "So I guess we have to somehow go back to square one. I admit, I'm at a loss where to begin."

"Can't you, like, *talk* to her? Get some information that way?" I studied the Sassy Suzy strip one last time before sealing it into the mailer. I irritated myself by constantly looking over my shoulder, expecting Eleanor to appear again.

"It doesn't usually work like that for me. I just get flashes... If we had the information that Mary found, we could do something with that. Maybe…" She paused and stared out at the dark night beyond the kitchen door as if the answers floated there. She moved the curtain. A warm wind buffeted me and I suddenly remembered something.

"Oh, my gosh, wait here a minute." I opened the door to the Bookmark and reached for the switch to flood the large room with light. Rummaging around behind the left-hand coffee bar, I recovered a box of random electronic things I had brought from the house in Garland. Among the wires of routers and other items rested Mary's BlackBerry. I lifted it and rummaged deeper for the charger cord.

"What's that?" Angie asked curiously when I closed the door behind me and took a seat at the dining table.

"Plug this in, will you?" I requested, handing her the cord.

She looked around until she found an outlet.

I pressed the power button and the data tool came to life. "I stopped phone service on this, but her address book and other info should still be here."

Angie's face lit with hope. "Oh, too cool!" she exclaimed, leaning to look over my shoulder.

I scrolled through Mary's address book, frustrated to find no Annalise listed. I switched screens and entered the application for various projects. Listed as bold as day, I found the title *Annalise and Eleanor*.

"Oh, my God, you were right," I said. "She *was* helping Eleanor."

Angie laughed with delight and kissed the top of my head. "Awesome! What does it say?"

I opened the application to find a list of brief notes. I saw references to New York and San Francisco, someone named Katherine Lyrian, Annalise Carter's name, and a phone number and an address in Berkeley.

"Do you think that's really her?" Angie asked.

"I'm not sure. It could be. I wonder who Katherine Lyrian is."

"Well, I'm sure she got married and had kids. This was the 1950s after all. Maybe Katherine is her child."

"Yep, that could be. But what if she identified as lesbian?" I tapped a fingernail thoughtfully against my bottom lip.

"I guess she could have still had kids."

"I dunno. We didn't do it so much back then like we do now." Angie agreed. "True. Well, should we call the number?"

"And say what? I'm a little nervous about that."

"Good point," Angie said, moving to place her empty cup in the sink. "Most people don't react well to 'Hello, I need to know what happened to Annalise Carter because the ghost of her dead lover is haunting me.'"

I studied her, waiting for her to acknowledge her own humor. She didn't, so I had to laugh at her seriousness. "Yep, I would imagine." I glanced at the clock and saw it was close to midnight. "Look, it's too late to call tonight anyway. Let's go to bed and get a fresh perspective in the morning."

Angie lifted her arms and yawned loudly. "Yeah, I have to work the morning shift at Mama's."

"So y'all are opening?"

"Yep, until the storm gears up. We'll have a few regulars who will still come out." She turned to me and pulled me to my feet. "Did I tell you how much I enjoyed our time together before Eleanor so rudely interrupted us?"

I felt my cheeks turning pink. "No, you didn't. Did you enjoy it as much as I did?"

"Hmm, I've forgotten," she mused, grinning. "Let's go over it again."

ANGIE

"Was that Donny's truck I saw dropping you off out there, Mama?" I asked.

She tucked her pocketbook into its usual slot under the dish rack and grinned at me. "And what if it was?"

I shrugged. "Just glad he's staying on this side of the water 'til the storm's over. That's all."

"Mmm-hmm." She glanced at the griddle where I stood. "What's that you're cooking?"

"Pancakes. For Grey."

Mama pulled on her apron. "Lord, child, don't you be cookin' for that girl. She'll run for the hills and won't give you the time of day even, ever again."

"Mama," I protested. "I can cook!"

She shooed me aside and took over the griddle. "Where is she anyway?" she asked.

"Walked over to the post office to mail in her comic strip." I stirred the batter after Mama checked it and added more milk.

"That's right, I forgot we have a celebrity in our midst. Butter these, will you?"

I slathered fresh butter on the first stack of pancakes and placed them in the warmer. "We always have celebrities coming through here, Mama. You know that."

"Yeah, but they don't stay. They don't live here."

"That software guy did. He built a mansion on the island," I pointed out.

"Um-hmm. So what's the latest on the ghost over there?" She nodded toward the Bookmark as she flipped a layer of pockmarked pancakes.

"We're getting to the bottom of it. It's someone attached to one of the books Grey's late partner owned."

She watched me curiously. "What does the ghost want?"

I explained the whole Eleanor and Annalise story, wrapping up just as Grey entered the kitchen. I pulled her close so I could talk in her ear. "We have pannacakes."

"Oh, good. I love pannacakes," she responded.

"Good answer."

Mama studied Grey and me. "I guess you'll be glad to be shed of that ghost finally. Angie tells me y'all have been having a time with it." She opened the refrigerator, took out a five-pound box of bacon, and started placing slices out on the meat griddle. A healthy sizzle filled the room.

"I will," Grey said, watching with interest as Mama worked. "I want to open the coffee shop, but am afraid to with all this activity going on. This ghost even plays in the public restrooms, throwing paper towels and unrolling the toilet tissue."

Mama and I both laughed at the admission.

"Well, we'd better go ahead and eat, sweetheart. We open in half an hour," I said.

As if hearing my thoughts, Gail entered through the back door and stopped dead still, surprised to see us all standing there.

"Well, good morning!" she said. "How is everybody on this stormy Monday?" She stood an umbrella near Mama's handbag and pulled her apron off the hook. "Have you opened up the front yet, Angie?"

I grinned at her. "No, ma'am, I've just been making pancakes."

Mama grunted.

I made a face at her.

"I'll bring breakfast," Grey said. "You go open the front with Gail."

I touched her hand. "Thank you, babe."

Gail and I busied ourselves with switching on the overhead lights and paddle fans, and preparing the dining room for the day even as good food started piling up on the bar. I went over to the front door and slid open the deadbolts. Almost immediately, the door rattled on its hinges as a gust of wind battered it.

"Gail," I called. "What are the wind speeds supposed to get to today?"

"About fifty miles per hour," she said, coming up behind me to peer at the leaden sky.

"How long do you think we should stay open?"

"You know that's up to Maylie, but I bet they close the bridge earlier than they said." Gail switched on the red neon OPEN sign situated in the window next to the door.

I walked over to the bar and took the plate Grey handed me. I helped myself to pancakes, bacon and warm syrup. Grey served her own plate and perched on the barstool next to me. Mama came through the kitchen door and I hailed her.

"No sense opening up, Mama. Wind's already thirty or better. I seriously doubt anyone's coming out."

Mama looked out the front windows where palm trees could be seen whipping about in a mad Dervish dance. "You might be right, baby girl. I'm here 'til noon though. That's when Donny's picking me up. Might as well stay open."

"You can close up, Mama. I'll run you home."

"In that wide open vehicle of yours? I don't think so. We'd never get out of the square in one piece." She smiled at me and stuffed her mouth with a forkful of pancake.

"Can you call him? Get him to come a little early? You don't want to be on the road when this wind gets up—"

"Now Angie, he's just picking up plywood in Brownsville. He'll be on directly."

"Mama!" I said insistently. "I'm serious. You and Gail need to hightail it out of here."

"Who died and made you the boss?" Mama growled, but she plucked her cell phone from her pocket and headed into the kitchen.

GREY

Later that day at my place, Angie and I had a simple dinner of sandwiches and chips, and discussed our childhoods while we waited for the storm to pass. Angie told me about how her mother, pregnant and alone, had made her way into South Texas riding a Greyhound bus from a small bayou town in deep south Louisiana. Maylie had saved money for her ticket by working in something called a crawdad kitchen. It was there that she learned about her talent for cooking.

After arriving in The Point, she waited tables and also worked as a cook in just about every restaurant around, living off one job and saving the money from the other. She lived frugally. To save money on child care, she took Angie to work with her when she could. Eventually, she fell into a good paying job at a place called Nonis which she bought and renamed The Fat Mother.

"Seems like I was born and bred in a kitchen," Angie joked.

"So you never knew your father. Did she ever tell you anything about him?"

She shook her head and took a swig of beer. "Not much. She says I have his hair and chin, and that he was her high school sweetheart."

"Why did they split up?"

"She never said exactly, but from what I overheard when I was younger, I think she walked in on him with another woman. So she left and never looked back."

"I wonder if he even knew about you," I mused.

"No clue." Angie shrugged. "Weird that Mama never married anyone. That kinda bugs me. I don't want Mama to grow old alone."

I shook my head. "She won't. We'll always be around. As long as she feeds us, that is." We had a good laugh over that one.

The power went out that night about eight o'clock. I have to admit to the terror that paralyzed me when the lights snapped off with such brutal suddenness. I just knew Eleanor was there, hovering, ready to strangle one of us.

Angie had expected this and came prepared. She quickly lit the dozen or so candles scattered about the apartment almost immediately, so I felt somewhat reassured. The flickering shadows offered their own menace, though. We huddled together on the sofa, trying to read and talking desultorily. The howling wind was deafening. Oscar Marie cowered in my arms, her claws alternately extending and relaxing as she kneaded my arm, seeking comfort.

"Should we go to sleep?" I offered finally when I'd had to read the same paragraph six times just to glean some meaning from it. I couldn't concentrate. There was a funny feeling to the apartment, a sense of electricity. I could tell Angie felt it too. I'd never seen her so jumpy. Was it just the lightning outside? Or was there something more sinister manifesting?

"As if," she answered. She slapped her book closed and rubbed her eyes. It was about that time that the storm growing inside mirrored perfectly the storm outside.

It started with the dishes in the kitchen cabinets. They began rattling at the same time as a sudden burst of thunder. I thought at first that the vibration of the thunder had caused the noise, but the sound continued even when the thunder abated.

Angie slowly stood. Oscar Marie squalled loudly and leapt from my arms to disappear behind the sofa. I rose to my feet just as a butcher knife dislodged from the knife block and whizzed past my head to stab into the wall behind me. I heard the twang of metal as it vibrated.

"Oh, no," whispered Angie. "The storm has given her strength!"

"Is it Eleanor?" I asked, eyeing the knife as it seesawed, its point buried in the wood.

"Yes," Angie hissed.

"What will she do to us?" My voice quavered.

Sudden repeated thuds against the door to the Bookmark set my heart racing. They were so hard, I felt them in the floorboards beneath my feet.

"I'm not sure," Angie answered when the sound quieted, "but I'm sure it won't be pleasant."

One by one, the kitchen cabinets creaked open. The doors stopped as if meeting resistance until each one was precisely aligned. Drawers opened. As I watched, the contents rose and hovered until a sharp wind appeared and swept them into a whirling spiral.

I knew this trick, had seen it before but with books.

"Get down," I screamed, just as a rain of kitchen implements shot out and made a beeline for us. Angie and I cowered on the floor, hiding our faces and heads as a curtain of lightweight metal draped across us. Some of the pieces stung and hit hard enough to draw blood.

A wail sounded, so loud that it thundered and echoed in the room. Unimaginably loud whispers sounded, one-sided conversations that actually tickled my eardrums. I clasped my hands over my ears and screamed, in fury or fear, I wasn't sure which. The attack continued until the items had been exhausted, but then saucepots and lids shot out from the bottom cupboards and crashed around the room in a volley of noise.

A wind swept by me. The stack of paper I kept in my drafting table went flying across the room to separate into individual wings that floated wounded to the floor. The drapes at the dining room window billowed and whipped around until I feared they would be pulled from their mooring. They subsided into stillness. All that I could hear was my hitching breath and the howling wind outside.

Angie stood and moved to the center of the room. She spoke in a loud, clear voice. "Eleanor. We know what you want. We are trying to find out what happened to Annalise for you. I swear. Just give us more time…"

A sudden scream ripped through the apartment. Angie went down as if she'd been bludgeoned. I screamed myself, remembering the day I'd seen Eleanor strangling Angie in the easy chair. A shadow darted across the room with mind-numbing speed, and the door to the Bookmark creaked open. All was still once more.

I crawled to Angie's side and discovered that she was alive, just dazed by the blow. Together, we knelt in the center of the floor and peered toward the door.

Suddenly, as we watched, a flame of light grew in the darkness near the center of the Bookmark. It formed into a round ball. As Angie and I gained our feet, it raced toward us. Only by leaping apart were we able to avoid being hit by it. The ball flickered and died before slamming into the wall behind us. Another ball grew and also streamed toward us from the darkness. Sounds of weeping carried to us as the storm whipped against the house from outside. Yet another spectral fireball came out of the darkness.

"I am so over this," Angie ground out.

Dodging the newest fireball, she leaned her weight against the door to the Bookmark, trying to close it and stop the attack. She almost succeeded, but just before she got it closed, the door slammed open again, sending her flying across the room, into the sofa and a coffee table. My heart stopped when I saw Angie's body crash down after being tossed like a rag doll. Tears sprang from my eyes and sobs tore from me. If I lost Angie too, my life would be over for certain.

Beginning at the top of my head, I felt like warm bathwater flowed across me. The sensation made me unable to breathe for an eon of seconds. Panic filled me. What new diabolical torture did Eleanor plan next? Yet this felt different somehow, so I stilled and waited, drawing on every ounce of forbearance I could muster. Out of the corner of my eye, I saw Angie crawl from the wreckage and shake herself. She spied my distress, my stillness, and she came to me.

"Your hair," she breathed. "It's...it's standing up. You're glowing."

I looked at her, saying goodbye with my eyes, sure that Eleanor was taking me with her. I felt no pain, only heat. I wanted to wipe away the trickle of blood on Angie's brow that threatened to invade one of her eyes, but my arms would not move. I realized that I could breathe but only shallowly, sipping tiny gulps of air.

Angie laid a hand against my forearm and closed her eyes.

"It's Mary," she whispered. "Mary is with you."

Tears sprang from my eyes only to be kissed away by heat.

A voice sounded in my head and I rose, somehow pulling Angie with me. We moved as one toward the Bookmark. When another fireball flashed into existence, we walked right into it unscathed.

Angie stumbled on the threshold, and we were free of Mary's weight. Angie pulled me into her arms and we pressed against the interior wall of the Bookmark.

As we watched, a glow began to fill the room. It started by the front windows. At first, I thought it came from the repeated lightning from outside, but this glow grew steadily, backlit by the flashes of lightning.

Then I saw her. I saw my Mary.

ANGIE

I saw Mary release Grey and move to the front of the room. Light emanated from her as she stood examining us with dark, unreadable eyes. Oddly, she was outlined in tiny points of light. Even her eyes and lips were outlined. I watched her spellbound. I studied her fingernails and the veins on the back of her hands, wondering at the tiny pricks of light that covered them. Her clothing was like a fabric made of miniscule stars.

"Isn't she beautiful," Grey said in a breathy voice.

I looked at her and followed her gaze. "You can see her?"

She nodded silently. We watched transfixed as Mary shimmered before us.

Then I saw Eleanor. She sat in one of the chairs near Mary. Her face was in her hands, and her long hair streamed over her hands and moved in a spectral wind as she rocked to and fro. I heard her sobs. The word *abandoned* came to me over and over again.

I pulled Grey against me, sensing a need to protect her from what would happen next.

Eleanor paused in her movements. She lifted her face from her hands. Her eyes, horrible in their vacant whiteness, fixed on Mary. Eleanor's scream rang through the room as she leapt on the other spirit, only to encounter a wall of light. She fell back, defeated, and flickered like a faulty diode. I felt fury rolling off her in waves. Books began to move on the shelves. Some broke free and whirled through the room, bullets of potential pain.

A slim, black-clad leg appeared next to Mary, as if stepping from behind a curtain. Eleanor stilled. Books crashed to the floor throughout the room. The curtain parted to reveal the slender body of a beautiful redhead. The woman stood with Mary in the capsule of light.

"Annalise," I whispered. Grey stirred in my arms. I knew she could see her as well.

Annalise moved closer to Eleanor. I saw her mouth move, but couldn't hear what was said. Eleanor must have heard, however. She smiled and changed subtly. *Annalise*. The word echoed through the room.

Annalise smiled and held out her hand. Eleanor reached through the glowing light this time. As their hands met, the entire room lit up like houselights in a darkened theater. The flash blinded me for a moment, but when I squinted and looked again, Annalise was home in Eleanor's arms. The two spirits faded into mist. Only Mary remained.

To my surprise, Grey broke free from my arms and raced to Mary. I gasped in horror and moved to catch her, only to have her shirt brush my fingertips as she moved away.

"Grey, don't leave me!" I cried hoarsely, stumbling after her.

Grey stopped at the capsule of light that surrounded Mary. They gazed at one another. I came up behind Grey, sobs building in my throat. If Grey chose to leave with Mary, my life would be over.

Grey lifted both hands and gently pressed them to the shimmering capsule. Mary smiled, the pinpoints of light moving and rearranging themselves.

I extended a hand, but drew it back, tears cascading down my cheeks. This was a decision Grey had to make alone.

Mary lifted both her glowing hands and pressed them to Grey's. I saw a watery membrane of light still separated their hands, which gave me faint hope.

They smiled at one another for a timeless instant. I saw something resolve between them. As one, Mary and Grey turned and looked at me.

Suddenly self-conscious, I swiped at my face and tried a lame smile. I realized suddenly that the light was dimming in subtle stages.

Mary stepped back, lowering her arms. She looked around the Bookmark. I saw approval register in her light-framed face. Her form flickered suddenly, and without a backward glance, she turned and stepped through an invisible curtain, pulling the capsule of light behind her.

Grey and I stood in the center of the darkened Bookmark. I was afraid to look at her, afraid I would see rejection, regret, things I did not want to see.

Instead, I looked out the front windows at the cloud swells lit by fragments of lightning. Grey's hand snaked into mine. I breathed again when she lifted my hand to her lips. I still couldn't look at her, afraid of losing complete control of my emotions. Grey seemed to sense my fragility. Side by side, we watched the roiling night together.

GREY

I knew how Angie must feel, having seen me and Mary together. I wanted so badly to explain to her how important an act of closure that had been, how I had needed it to move on to my new life with her. Words failed me, however. My feelings ran too deep to verbalize.

Instead, I took her hand. After some time regaining our composure, I led her from the Bookmark and back into the apartment. Chaos met my gaze. I shut the door firmly behind us. I turned the lock when I saw Oscar Marie perched safely on the dining table.

Angie moved to tidy up, but I shook my head, letting her know it could wait.

She followed me down the hall to the bedroom.

We silently prepared for bed. Lying next to one another, we still didn't talk, just stared at the ceiling as light from distant lightning played across it.

Angie was the first to break the silence.

"I almost lost you," she said simply.

I felt the hidden power of those words. "Never," I said, pulling her into my arms. I nestled her weight atop me and looked up into her sapphire gaze. "I'm yours, Angie. In this world and the next. Promise me you will remember that."

She nodded. Salty tears dropped from her eyes to moisten my cheeks. I kissed her, and was once again transported to that warm, secure place of loving Angie.

Her hands against my head felt so right. She rained tender kisses along my face and neck. We moved together, our bodies straining for loving touches. As she unbuttoned my shirt and her kisses moved lower, I realized with joy that we were indeed completely alone together. At last.

ANGIE

I stared at the ruins of my school and felt pretty close to tears. Grey took my hand and silently held it, offering comfort. I sure had been on quite the emotional roller coaster of late.

"Maybe it's for the best," I said finally. "They were going to tear it down anyway. Now the fight is over and I have to say, I feel some sense of relief."

"No, you don't," she replied, turning around so she could stare at the bay instead of the broken building. "You're worried about the kids."

I released her hand and walked to the front door. It gaped widely, the lock broken. Torrential rain and wind had finally done in the old building, shredding the roof like the talons of a giant eagle. Most of the asphalt roofing tiles lay broken on the swollen wooden floorboards.

I stepped inside carefully, trying to see what I could salvage. The walls of the main room were rain soaked and drooping. I was glad I had taken down all the artwork and the teaching aids before the storm. At least we had saved those. I saw the destroyed bookcase and was equally glad the books and workbooks had been tucked safely away.

"Wow, this is pretty bad," Grey said. "We really need to get the stuff and go, sweetheart. I'm worried about this floor. It took a lot of rain."

I sighed and turned to her. "Yeah, you're right. There isn't much left in here anyway."

We backtracked and entered my office. A beam had fallen across my old desk and the entire office was soaked. Working together, we were able to free the plastic bins and the locked safe. On the way out, I gently disengaged the sign David had made for me. Miraculously, it was intact with water damage on one corner only.

We loaded the Jeep. Just as I started the engine, I spied a metal square resting diagonally across the stone foundation. I hopped out of the Jeep. Lifting it, I saw that it was the Petey Wilson plaque that had hung next to the doorway. I tapped it with my knuckles, profound grief washing through me.

I stood and took a deep breath, pushing the grief away. In life, there were always beginnings and endings, and this was just one more. We'd find a new place and everything would be just fine once again. I believed that.

Handing the plaque to Grey for safekeeping, I swung myself into the Jeep and we headed home.

GREY

The strip was coming along nicely.

I got a new cookbook, Sassy Suzy told her co-worker Rita.

Oh, yeah? Rita replied. *Made anything good?*

Nope, I think I'm gonna take it back.

Really? Are the recipes too hard?

No, just impossible. Each one tells me to start with a clean dish.

***

I leaned back and stretched as I listened intently. It was way too quiet in the front. I lifted my coffee cup and stood. I needed a refill anyway.

My phone vibrated in my pocket, so I fished it out and saw a text from Couscous. It was time. Excitement raced through me as I pressed a speed dial number and got the padre, who was waiting with the bus outside.

We talked briefly. I stepped into the Bookmark where I was inundated with the delicious scents of flavored coffee and fresh pastry. Half a dozen chairs were filled. I waved to a few regulars who lifted their heads as I made my way across the room.

The reading room had been growing in popularity during the past year, and was strangely well liked by both the local retirees as well as the college students from UTB.

I had been a little taken aback. As expected, the spring breakers from last year hadn't been interested in the books, but the coffee and pastries had proven a surprising draw. The Winter Texans had fallen in love with the place as a social gathering spot. Their word of mouth brought in a daily rise in customers this past October. Now here it was, spring again, and I'd had to put in a real cash register and hire two employees, one full-time and one part-time.

My part-time employee, Maria, motioned me over. I paused by the coffee bar.

I studied her cautiously smiling face and was again amazed by her transformation since graduating from the SPICEY last fall. She still wore her hair long and swept to the side to hide her scarred face, but now she smiled most of the time and had become something of an expert on rare books. She also kept the Bookmark's inventory squeaky clean.

"Hey, *chica*, you doing okay?" I asked.

She nodded. "I am. How's the strip coming?" I made a dismissive gesture and she laughed. "Listen, Forrest took home *San Francisco Blues*. I told him it was okay," she said.

"Oh, sure, that's fine. He always returns them." I cocked my head to one side, trying to remember the book.

"It's Kerouac," she said, grinning.

"I sure am glad you know what you're talking about," I said. "Did you enter it in the borrowed list on the machine?"

"I did."

I leaned close and spoke softly. "It's time. We'll be back in just a few hours. You call me if you need anything." I glanced at the clock on the wall behind her. "Jackson will be here in, oh, about half an hour."

Maria covered her mouth to stem an excited squeal. "Oh, my gosh, this is so cool," she sighed. "Take some pictures so I can see?"

"Will do, sweetie."

I approached the closed double doors to the eastern half of the Bookmark and paused before opening them. Hearing about Jack Kerouac made me think about Eleanor. I almost missed her presence, and might have liked having her around if she hadn't tried to take out her anger and frustration on Angie and me. I sighed and pushed open both doors.

Sound inundated me. I quickly closed the doors. At first, I didn't see Angie, but her tousled blond hair popped up behind one of the easy chairs. She saw me and grinned.

"Angie? What are you doing?" I asked.

"Sally won't come out."

I frowned. "Come out? Come out from where?"

"She's behind the chair," Tommy said, appearing next to me.

I turned back to Angie. "Um, rough day teaching, Ange?"

"Don't you give me 'tude," she said, rising to her feet. "Everything was fine until this one," she indicated Tommy, "decided that Sally's letters weren't written the right way."

I turned to the teen and gave him the stink eye. "Tommy, maybe you should be the one getting Sal out…with an apology."

Tommy sighed dramatically, as though everyone in the world had it in for him today. He went over to the chair and loudly apologized. He looked at me a moment later. "It ain't working," he informed me.

"*Isn't* working," Angie and Emma Rachel said in unison.

I looked at both of them and had to laugh. I walked over to the chair and crouched until I could see a pouting, tearful Sally huddled behind it. "Hey, Sally, wanna go for a ride?"

She peered up at me. I saw excitement stir in her eyes. "Where?" she asked.

"It's a surprise," I whispered.

"Can Piggy go?" she asked, holding out the stuffed bedraggled Muppet character that had become her constant companion since the school had been destroyed in the storm.

I nodded very seriously. "Oh, yes, I should think so." I helped her from behind the chair to scattered applause from Tommy and the other students.

"Okay, field trip time, everyone!" I announced, moving to the table and neatening up workbooks and other the lesson supplies. I met Angie's concerned gaze.

"Beach trip?" she asked in a low voice. "We have a test Friday."

I cupped her chin in my hand and shook it gently. "It'll be okay," I assured her. "Trust me."

A knock sounded on the outside door. Emma Rachel rushed to unbolt it and let in Father Sephria. Angie looked from the padre back to me, and I could see her mind working, trying to figure out my game. Shrugging, she obviously decided to play along and began readying Delicia's wheelchair for the trip.

Following Angie's example, Emma Rachel began working on Connie's wheelchair, even as she signed to Carter and Emilio so they would understand what was happening.

I walked over to Frederick's bed and found him sleeping. Gabby looked up at me from the magazine she was reading.

"We'll bring back photos from the trip," I told her. "I hope he won't feel left out if he wakes up while we're gone."

"I doubt he'll wake," she said in her softly accented English. "He was up most of the night. Couldn't settle down."

I nodded. "We won't be gone too long. I think he'll be pleased when he finds out where we went."

ANGIE

It was really unusual for Grey to interrupt classes, so I was mighty curious what she had up her sleeve. If it had been closer to mealtime, I would have expected a surprise meal out. She'd done that before, but this was early afternoon. I admit I was pretty well bewildered. Yet I trusted her and went along eagerly.

As if I wouldn't do anything for Grey Graham. After seeing the collapsed roof on the SPICEY building after the storm last year, she had moved us right into the Bookmark without blinking an eye. She dealt with the noise, the aggravation, the bus taking over her alley parking space, and the reduction of her business footage without a cross word. She had definitely taken the SPICEY under her wing. For that alone, I would be eternally grateful.

To my surprise, the bus turned right instead of left toward the island. I figured it had to be a shopping excursion, or we were going out for an ice cream treat. As if confirming my suspicions, in just a few short minutes we pulled into the parking lot of the local Dairy Queen. I started to raise a cheer, but to my surprise, the padre continued on through the parking lot and into the lot next to it.

Then I saw the signs, and sudden hot tears blurred my vision. The long, rigid signs above both front and side doors, artfully designed in bright primary colors, proclaimed *The South Padre Island Center for Extraordinary Youth*.

I rose and moved forward while the bus pulled to a stop in front of the double doors at the side entrance. The padre chuckled as he swung open the bus door. I practically fell down the steps and out of the bus.

Looking like ants abandoning a waterlogged anthill, Couscous's family poured through the doors. I also saw Sanchez, who came up and gave me a big hug. Cathy was there with Stephanie, and I saw Melissa, who waved and gestured with an uncharacteristic thumbs-up sign. Bringing up the rear of the group came big, old, lumbering Couscous and my dear Mama, both beaming as they shared in my joy.

"How...but how?" was the extent of my brilliance as I was surrounded by all the people I cared so much about.

Sensing my dilemma, Mama came over to me. "It was all Grey's idea, honey. She approached Couscous and he got this little piece of land for a song, or so he says."

"I made the owner an offer he couldn't refuse," Couscous said, causing a ripple of hilarity to break across the crowd.

I was too shell-shocked for laughter. I looked back toward the bus where Grey was helping Emma Rachel and the padre unload the kids from the hydraulic platform at the back.

Emilio ran up to me and lifted me off the ground in his exuberance. He put me down and ran off into the building, followed by Carter, Stevie and the rest of the group.

I glanced back and saw Grey watching me. I caught her eyes and tried to thank her with my gaze, but there were so many tears, it was tough going. She shooed me away, motioning for me to go inside. I lowered my face and shook my head, knowing I wouldn't even be able to talk if I went up to her right now.

Shy and confused, Sally moved to me and buried her face in my stomach. She held her Piggy doll tightly pressed to her chest. I took her hand and we went inside together.

She abandoned me almost immediately because the long table in the center of the big room was loaded with a huge sheet cake and four tubs of ice cream. It was under siege by a horde of young people as Melissa and Sanchez tried to serve everyone. Grey and the padre pushed Connie and Delicia over to the table and pitched in to help.

"That's quite a woman you got there," said Couscous. He had taken a seat near the doorway. His ham-like hands were folded together atop the curve of his ornate walking stick.

"How?" I asked, again showing my brilliant use of language.

Couscous laughed and shrugged. "She called me when the roof went on the old building. Said we needed a place for the kids and for you to teach. We been working on it ever since. She hired some architect to design it and brought in some company from McAllen to build it." He looked across the room. "I think they did a good job."

I swiped at my eyes and took a good look around, something I hadn't taken the time to do yet. The huge common room had been divided into four quadrants, each filled with new school furniture, solid functional pieces waiting to be used by students.

I looked up and noted that they had installed accordion-style room dividers that could be pulled into place via tracks set into the twelve-foot high ceiling. One quadrant, closest to the double doors in the far wall, had been made into a cafeteria, already equipped with tables and chairs, items that were fast taken over by those who had been served ice cream and cake.

To my right, toward the back of the building, were two restrooms with wide doorways and handicap access signs. Beyond them, three gaping doorways which were no doubt offices.

I found my voice finally. "This is just incredible," I said softly. "I passed this building just about every day, and every time I saw it, I just assumed it was another real estate office being built. I never even guessed. Amazing."

"Hey, I been meaning to ask you. How come my kids ain't extraordinary?"

Confused, I turned to him. "What's that?"

"This place," he indicated the building. "For extraordinary youth. Ain't my kids extraordinary?"

I corrected him automatically. "Aren't. And of course they are."

He shrugged expressively. "So how come they can't go here?"

I studied him, thinking about the requirements for the charter school, how they might have to be altered. My mind expanded with new options, new challenges. "Of course they can go to school here. Do you want them to?"

"I do." He nodded slowly. "Make it happen."

I chuckled. "Okay. I will."

Grey carried over a large bowl filled with cake and ice cream and handed it to Couscous.

"So I can surmise that you are pleased?" she asked me coyly.

"Oh, you don't even know the half of it," I replied.

"Come see the offices," she said, taking my hand and pulling me along the hallway. "By the way, Couscous says you can own the land, if you want, just by paying him one hundred dollars a month."

"Man, you guys are unbelievable. How will I ever pay *you* back?"

She paused in her headlong rush to look at me with questioning eyes. "Why, you already have, honey. Anyway, I thought you'd like this office best," she said, stepping through the first door on the right. "We got you a new desk and everything."

I looked through the door, focusing on the framed and mounted shadow box bearing the metal plaque we had rescued from the old school building. I almost choked up again.

Grey glanced at me, then turned and pointed out the window. "You can see the bay from this window here and know we're looking at the same scenery each day."

I noted that someone had framed David's sign and hung it to the right of the doorway. I touched it, then closed the door and moved to stand close behind Grey at the window. I wrapped my arms around her waist and pressed my face to her sweet-smelling hair.

"It'll be strange being away from you for so many hours at a time," I murmured, sighing.

She turned in my arms and pensively studied my face. "But we'll always have the nights," she said with impish delight.

I kissed her thoroughly, taking my time as I curved her pliant body into mine. "Oh yes, there are always the nights," I whispered against her lips.